**Tim Hesitated. Then He Knocked Gently. He Was Proud Of Himself. He Wanted To Kick The Door In, But He Only Knocked Gently.**

She called, "Come in."

He would, he would. He opened the door and stepped inside, standing straight, powerful and male. There she stood.

"Is there something you need?" Carol asked politely.

*Oh, yes . . .* he thought. "I'll come back later."

Coolly she replied, "I have appointments today. Perhaps another time." She was piqued.

Tim smiled, as if he were looking at a dog that was showing its teeth and snarling. "Perhaps tomorrow," he said gently.

And as any man almost thirty has learned to do— and as any Chicago police detective knows especially well to do—he exited.

Dear Reader,

Welcome to August! As I promised last month, August's *Man of the Month* title is by one of your favorites—and mine—Diana Palmer. It's called *Night of Love,* and this story really is something wonderful and special.

The rest of August is equally terrific. First, there's *Kane's Way* by Dixie Browning. You know, it's hard to believe that this talented lady has written over *fifty* books for Silhouette! And they all just keep getting better and better.

Next comes a fun-filled story from Lass Small. The title of Lass's latest is *Balanced,* but I'm not sure that our hero and heroine feel exactly "balanced" for most of the book . . . more like *off*-balanced from love.

The month is completed by delightful, sensuous, sparkling stories from Cathie Linz, Linda Turner and Barbara McCauley. And as for September, well, have we got some great stuff in store for you. Look for new series by Ann Major *and* Joan Hohl, as well as some delightful tales from four other fabulous writers.

So, until next month, happy reading.

Lucia Macro
Senior Editor

# LASS SMALL
## BALANCED

SILHOUETTE *Desire*®
Published by Silhouette Books New York
**America's Publisher of Contemporary Romance**

 SILHOUETTE BOOKS
300 East 42nd St., New York, N.Y. 10017

BALANCED

Copyright © 1993 by Lass Small

All rights reserved. Except for use in any review, the reproduction or utilization of this work in whole or in part in any form by any electronic, mechanical or other means, now known or hereafter invented, including xerography, photocopying and recording, or in any information storage or retrieval system, is forbidden without the permission of the publisher, Silhouette Books, 300 E. 42nd St., New York, N.Y. 10017

ISBN: 0-373-05800-4

First Silhouette Books printing August 1993

All the characters in this book have no existence outside the imagination of the author and have no relation whatsoever to anyone bearing the same name or names. They are not even distantly inspired by any individual known or unknown to the author, and all incidents are pure invention.

® and ™:Trademarks used with authorization. Trademarks indicated with ® are registered in the United States Patent and Trademark Office, the Canada Trade Mark Office and in other countries.

Printed in the U.S.A.

## LASS SMALL

finds living on this planet at this time a fascinating experience. People are amazing. She thinks that to be a teller of tales of people, places and things is absolutely marvelous.

To my son,
William Kelly Small,
who lived with mice

# One

Timothy Bolt was twenty-nine years old and an un-married orphan. He was a pleasantly plain man who was tall enough at almost six feet, and he was nicely built. He had brown hair and startlingly green eyes. He was a detective on the Chicago Police Force.

On the particular spring day when it all began, Tim was especially tired and a little cross. The whole day had been a nasty mess. He had a cut on his cheek, and his stomach hurt from a head punch he'd not been able to avoid.

Back at the station, he finished his report, carried it to his captain's desk and clumped tiredly to his cubicle.

On Tim's desk, in Ula's neat handwriting, the note read: "Call Mr. Brown at this number." Brown. Brown. Now that was a nothing name. Tim sat down at his desk and scowled at the wall. He sighed with forbearance and dialed the number. It was the Palmer House, the elegant hotel in downtown Chicago. Skeptically, he asked for Mr. Brown.

In the rasp of his long-ago injured voice, Salty Brown of Temple, Ohio, said, "Tim. Ah, your voice is just like your dad's. How're ya doing?"

"Salty?"

"Yeah."

"Are you here in town?"

"Yeah. You free for supper?"

"I hope to God you're doing the cooking."

And Salty laughed.

So they met and shared dinner at the Palmer House. They visited and caught up on each other, and Salty said, "I miss your dad just about as much as you do."

"He left a big, empty space in my life."

"It happens that way."

They talked about Sammy Bolt and what a perfect father and friend he'd been. "He was the damnedest stubbornest man I've ever known." And "My God, he was so thickheaded, nothing penetrated." And "He never did get over being seasick. You'd think a sailor would've adjusted. They offered for him to go ashore, but naturally, the land they picked was Korea."

And gradually, Salty got around to what he wanted. He said, "I know you developed a dislike for women after Pauline booted you. You'd be just right for what I need."

"Some woman bothering you?"

"Naw. My daughter, Carol, is bound and determined to live in Chicago, free and clear of family. She's special. Without any intention, she attracts men who're sometimes determined. You know? Would you be kind enough to live in an apartment in the same building and pretend to be aloof while you guard her?"

"What'd'ya have in mind?"

"I'll pay your bed and board while you keep an eye on her. You've always wanted to write, and this could be your chance. It'd give you an excuse to be around all day, and you can see if you can write The Great American Novel."

"I write horror stories."

Salty could see the parallel. "That pretty well describes just about what's been happening here in this country. The whole world's in flux. With all that, Carol needs somebody around I can count on. It's you. Will you?"

Tim had had to cope with pushy women. This woman was Salty's daughter. What sort of problem would she be? He said to Carol's hard-nosed genetic contributor, "Some women tend to drift into the wrong beds. What if she does?"

"Not Carol. She's an artist. A good one. She isn't ready to fool around with any man just for the experience."

"Daddies always say that."

Salty laughed. "Wait until you meet her. She's a dedicated woman. She'll gather people just like her mama, and she'll nurture them all, but she isn't ready to settle down or experiment. I know Carol."

"I won't be responsible for anything but her safety."

"That's all I ask. The windows will be reinforced and wired. There'll be a security alarm. We're getting all the things done ahead of time so she won't suspect we're interfering."

Tim grumbled a bit as he shifted around in his chair, but he finally admitted, "I would like the chance to try writing. I think I can."

Salty encouraged him. "It's an ideal opportunity. She's a lady. While she's tenderhearted and susceptible to woeful situations, she won't be stupid or unreasonable. You just have to be careful of her impulsive good Samaritanism. Protect her from lechers and strays."

"I can handle it."

Salty's rasp was kind. "I wouldn't've asked you if I hadn't known you could. You're like your dad. Just don't tell her I hired you. She thinks she can handle anything by herself."

Tim groaned. "Those kind are the ones that attract trouble."

And Salty nodded in agreement.

The next day the two went to see the apartment. It was located in an old house somewhat west and a little bit north of the center of the city and not too far from the lake. The area was in transition and not entirely residential.

The house had a deep basement, which held a printing shop. It wasn't noisy but when the machines were going full tilt, there was a little tremor in the structure.

Tim's own place had already been rented by Salty. It was on the second floor, just above Carol's downstairs apartment. The main staircase went along the other side of her living room wall and up the center of the house. The entrance hall at the bottom of the stairs had been left unaltered. Its coat closet held the house vacuum cleaner, a stubborn washer and a passable dryer.

"I've noticed a couple of mice," Salty mentioned. "It'll take everyone in the building to make a concerted effort to get rid of them."

"She scared of mice?"

"Carol? Naw. She doesn't 'see' them. If she doesn't actually look at them, she thinks they'll go away."

So Tim settled in. His apartment was sufficient. The bed was wide and the mattress was comfortable and suspiciously new. Tim figured Salty had purchased it and had it switched for the actual ratty, stained, mess that had occupied the rusty bedstead.

But Tim refrained from mentioning the bed to Salty in his weekly reports. He just enjoyed the luxury. It was the perfect bed. Well, almost.

He had a simple computer and printer. There was a stack of boxes with computer paper. He had sharpened pencils in a can nearby. His notes were impaled on a nail board that was alongside the computer. And he was ready.

He tapped on the keyboard and watched the screen as he saw the green letters stretch out: "It was a dark and stormy night . . ."

Did every writer begin that way in a salute to word-age?

He pressed the key to blink out the words and began: "Chapter One." Then he left his hands idle on the keyboard as he looked at those two words. He smiled because his mind had known the opening paragraph for a long time.

He had begun.


With some anticipation, he waited for his charge to move in downstairs. Salty had shown Tim a snapshot of a laughing, squint-eyed beanpole, with her hair in banded clumps poking out from her head. She looked very young for a college graduate. Under the bulky clothes, her figure wasn't defined at all. He was braced to deal with a wide-eyed innocent up from the sticks to the Big City.

While he'd waited for Carol to move in, Tim had checked out the other people in the divided-up house.

Two men lived in the apartment on the other half of the first floor. One was mental and a budding stockbroker. The other was a poet.

Sharing the second floor with Tim was an ageing actress. She had gone by the name of Gaye Desire as an ingenue, but she had changed her name to Thelma Wilson. She still aspired to the theater and did bit parts now and again.

There were four grad students who held the attic. They were the right age to be a problem for a single woman of means.

The attic occupants gave parties about every weekend. They always invited everyone in the house because they had bring-your-own-beer parties. But the invited ones who didn't show up could hardly complain about the noise.

Tim's first contact with Carol Brown had rocked him back on his heels. She wasn't anything like the snapshot Salty had shown him. She was so smooth and wise that she...intimidated him. Him? A Chicago police detective? She did.

She made Tim feel like a fifteen-year-old on his first try for a date.

The only thing about her and him that matched was they both had green eyes. She had naturally streaked blond hair to his dark hair. He was taller and male. She was—female. And she had been formed by some god who'd been an expert on how to build women's bodies.

She didn't act like she'd been a product of the Brown fortune but was only a struggling artist with no means. She wasn't living on daddy's money?

She appeared to believe she was a normal woman. She didn't strut or pose or smile at Tim enticingly. She didn't take off her clothes and ask him: Why wait? She looked at him as if she need not recognize him especially. She was courteous. How rude that was. And he was disgruntled.

But the really baffling part was that Carol didn't appear to notice she was remarkable. Or that he was a susceptible male and not too tacky. She irritated the hell out of him by being . . . courteous.

She didn't chat with him. She didn't seek him out to confide her fears and tremblings so that he could be brave and strong and protect her . . . from whatever. Anything at all.

She went about her business of drawing and shopping for materials and going God only knew where all outside his range of protection so that he was distracted from his writing.

She frustrated him.

At night, in his solitary bed, his libido dreamed she had a secret desire for him and she was coming up the stairs to him. She would open his locked door with just a gentle gesture of her hand and stand, staring at him, breathing brokenly with her need for him. She would remove the soft lace thing that barely covered her naked body, and she would come to his bedside.

Her short, streaked blond hair would become waist-length and gently waved. She would look down at him, her lips parted, her eyes luminous with her lust. She would tauntingly lift the sheet back from his bare body and look at him, her lips opening with her gasp of pleasure. Then she would crawl into his bed and all over him. No foreplay.

He would scold her for that. He would say, "You animal."

And she would laugh low in her throat and do something outrageous with her fingers.

He would say, "You're just using me."

And her savoring moan would agree.

Tim really didn't sleep well. That was why he changed his sweaty, tangled sheets so often and why he got up so early to jog all over the area. He attributed the sheet changing to tidiness and the jogging to getting to know the neighborhood and its people. Any good cop did that.

At first Carol had been evasive about his neighborly offer for her to call on him if she ever needed some help.

Tim had finally solved that through negotiations with Thelma. Thelma was such an independent woman that she had initially replied, "I'm a city woman. I can take care of myself. However, you are very kind to offer. Thank you. But I doubt seriously that I would ever need you."

After waiting a discreet while, Tim then suggested to Thelma, "You might mention to Miss Brown that I've offered to be your in-house guard. I've offered any help I can give to her, but I think she thinks I'm trying to come on to her."

Thelma considered, as she watched Tim's honest, open-faced look of concern, and she agreed to do that.

So what did Carol do? Had she immediately offered for Tim to move into her apartment and sleep with her to protect her from the bogeyman and the night horrors? No. She had him move furniture and shelves and boxes of heavy paper and deliver unwieldy pictures to clients.

She didn't really even notice him.

Tim had realized almost right away that Carol was a careful and prolific artist. She drew and painted meticulously. Her drawings and compositions were a part of her inner self. She was beginning to sell her works. She confessed the sales gave her mixed feelings. She loved each work and hated to let it go.

Tim thought it was too bad she wasn't a writer. While the writer shared the story, he could still keep it.

The stately old house was not too far from Lake Michigan. As does anyone who lives near any size of freshwater pond, the Chicago inhabitants referred to it as: The Lake.

Lake Michigan is the one that looks like the trunk of the humongous palm tree that makes up the Great Lakes at the top of the U.S. of A.

On one evening, Tim was a guest at a gathering in Carol's apartment. Tim listened as Carol claimed that in just seeing a map of the northern hemisphere and the very obvious Great Lakes, one could wonder if the graceful blue palm-tree image had been the whim of some remarkable race. A people who had lasered out that identifying brand in order to mark this continent as the paradise of this planet.

"Of course," she said, "the experts have declared the Great Lakes were created by the erosion of the glaciers, but those are the ponderous opinions of literals who are without imagination.

"Notice how the leaves are defined," Carol pointed out the lakes on the world map laminated on her wall. "That isn't happenstance."

"Ummmm," were the cautious replies of her guests.

"Or," Carol continued, "such an obvious marking could have been a code for flybys so that the flying saucers could check their planet maps. Maybe that's why they come here now and then. They might have war games, and we're a pylon for the path of flight.''

Tim watched as her visitors glanced at the map and made sounds that were noncommittal. Then they asked, ''Why do you have the map on this wall?''

''I have family almost all over everywhere.''

''Really?'' And they probably wondered why she had limited her map to just this world. Not that Carol was strange, but she was not—ordinary.

''For a while, my brother, Mike, was in the Persian Gulf, so his pin was there.'' She pointed.

''He okay?''

She smiled. ''Great. Mike and his new wife are down in Texas right now. So here's his double pin down there with the double one for Cray and his wife. There's Tweed, John and Tom. There's my sister, Georgia's, double pin in Indianapolis. And you can see that Fort Wayne, Indiana, has two doubles. Those are Rod's and Mitchell's families.''

A new acquaintance did mention, ''There're a lot of pins.''

Carol replied, ''There are a lot of us.''

The doubter inquired, ''Cousins and other relatives?''

And Carol replied gently, ''No, these are the siblings. The two big pearl pins, here in Ohio, represent my parents.''

The newcomer felt free to mention, ''No one has that many kids.''

''Well, some are adopted and some are actual and some were take-ins. You can have no idea how Cray moved around at one time. Tweed's pin was almost as restless, but he at least stayed on one continent.''

Tim observed the magic speaker. The ... pin ... had been restless. Uh-huh.

Back at the map, taking up the original cause for forming the Great Lakes, Carol continued with her theory: "The builders had to put the palm of lakes up here. All the other places either had water-absorbing sand or there wasn't enough water or the climate was too dry and the water would evaporate. To be scanned from space, the mark had to be obvious and constant.

"They probably had to do a lot of testing to find a way to keep the lakes blue and therefore filled with water. The land, here, isn't sand. Without the blue marking, the excavations could explain other slashes that mar our earth."

Tim saw that her listeners were tolerant. They nodded and murmured something neutral as they moved to look at her paintings.

Carol was a stunning painter.

When anyone saw her pictures, their lips would part in recognition of something they needed. They would stand and look at the figure or scene in darts and stares trying to absorb it quickly, unbelievingly.

Some painters capture a moment and keep it there forever. Those viewing know that when they came back to it, the same picture would be there. None of Carol's work was static. It felt alive like something caught briefly that could very possibly move, or subtly change. So the viewer's eyes had to stare for the moment in which her picture could still be seen, as it was then.

Gradually, Tim understood that Carol believed she and her works were perfectly ordinary. But there were others who appeared to be as unsettled as Tim about Carol.

Once a silent Tim heard one of her clients ask, "How do I know what those two will do when I'm not watching?" Tony asked that suspiciously of Carol's stunning, almost life-sized watercolor of Harlequin and Columbine who were standing, smiling at each other in a very knowing way.

Carol replied, "Good grief, Tony! It's paint on paper!"

"No." He was sure. "It isn't," he told her. "They're real."

"Are you smoking that stuff again?" she demanded.

And Tim didn't blink. Carol knew full well that Tony was clean. And so did Tim.

Tony pretended to become cross. "No, I'm pure. And you know it, you harpy."

"Leave the picture here. If it spooks you, I'll give you your money back."

"I haven't paid you yet. You're pushing for the check. I really don't care what they do. It's just that those two make me feel left out."

And she laughed.

Tony exclaimed, "See? That laugh is what you get in your pictures!"

She scoffed. "A laugh doesn't show up on paper."

"It does on your paintings," Tony assured her. "Look at his smile. You *know* what she just said. Look at her face. Just see that sly look on her blushing face."

"You're reading things into the picture I never put there."

"You must be a terror. Does any man trust you enough to try with you?"

"No."

"You can't possibly prefer women?"

She laughed a bubbling laugh that she tried to smother.

Then Tony asked, "When are you going to finally fall in love?"

Tim watched intensely as she shrugged, smiling a little, but her face was a bit sad.

Tony's voice was kind. "You loved that guy, Tweed, didn't you."

Tim's mind echoed silently: TWEED?

Carol replied pensively, "Yeah. But I wasn't the one. He never could see me."

Tim was still thinking: Tweed BROWN?

Tony questioned, "He's still single?"

"Yes."

"Want to try with me?"

Tim's muscles stiffened.

Carol declined. "Thank you, but we're too similar. We'd never have any conflicts that would be healthy and help us to mature. You need a different woman. Someone more...stable. You have to know I'm stable enough, but I wouldn't be good for you."

And ignoring the silent Tim as if he were harmless, Tony had the gall to suggest to Carol, "We could experiment. It might work."

Tim's breathing picked up and he tightened his mouth.

Carol dismissed such a thing. "You're just bored right now or you wouldn't even suggest it."

Tony sighed. "Yeah. You're right. When you're more stable, mention it, and I'll see if I can fit you in."

She exclaimed, "So generous!" But she didn't sound sincere.

"When do I get the picture?"

"It'll be about two weeks before it can be properly framed."

"I'm having a party next week. Could we wrap my picture in plastic and put a barrier up so no one will touch it?"

"Okay."

He beamed at the figures. "I want to show it off."

She guessed, "You're trying to get the price down with flattery."

"I'd like to pay double—I won't, of course—but I'd like to in order to get you out of this rat hole."

"Mouse hole." She corrected. "It's mice that have overrun the place."

"Are they still using the bed as a trampoline?"

"Come see."

Tony looked around as he strolled after Carol, and Tim followed in a silent but formidable manner. He knew Tony was aware of him because Tony was so casual in his movements.

Tony strolled along, looking at the stunning decorations on the high ceilings. They were not plaster, but actually carved wood. Carol had painted them as they must once have been. They were really lovely.

Carol's portion of the house had once been a living-drawing room and the butler's pantry was her kitchen. The hall to the kitchen, her bedroom and bath had once been the dining room. The doors were tall and slid back into the walls on top runners, which still worked.

The north-facing, windowed half of the living room was her studio. There were cupboards and shelves and two drawing tables. There were easels and stools and pots of upside-down brushes. There were trays and tubes of paint, and the place smelled somewhat of turpentine.

Separating her studio and the sitting-room space, Carol had set four, eight-foot, free-standing panels of material on which she'd creweled Erica Wilson's patterns. The panels were of the four seasons and simply gorgeous. They were so intricate that one could stare and find another bird or a butterfly or a gnat in the leaves of the season's trees. Everything was half yarn and half background material. It was very clever.

With their tagalong escort, the pair came to Carol's bedroom. The large iron curlicued bed was sitting grandly high and the bedding was tucked carefully under the mattress. Each tall bed leg had a version of the squirrel baffler used on bird feeders.

Tony shook his head. "What do your cats do?"

"They leap on the bed and safely watch the baffled mice."

Tony laughed.

Somewhat pensively, Carol mentioned, "I had to give away the canary. I loved to hear him sing, but he shared the seeds."

"I don't see how you can live here."

"It's inspiring. Come look."

With Tim shadowing them, she led Tony back to her studio and showed him pencil drawings of the cats and mice together. The cats were fascinated, the mice pragmatic and running about their business.

Tony chided, "Those cats aren't earning their keep."

"They weren't raised by a mouser. Mousing isn't an instinct, it's a learned talent."

"I couldn't live here."

"I would bet you have mice. You just don't mind."

"I'll check."

"Speaking of checks..."

"Okay. Okay! What a nag."

Carol promised that Tim would deliver the watercolor in time for Tony's party. She did glance at Tim for confirmation, and he solemnly nodded.

After Tony had left, Tim lingered unobtrusively so he got to watch as Carol went to stand sadly before the painted Harlequins. Obviously, she loved them. Why did it make her so pensive to look on the lovers?

Tim had been present as Carol had invited Thelma to go with her to Temple, Ohio, to meet her mother Felicia. Tim was so intrusive that it was with some irony that Carol invited him to go along. He declined with great reluctance. Since Carol didn't know why he was in the house, he didn't dare go face Salty and try to appear surprised.

The trip hadn't been successful. Carol had thought Thelma would enjoy meeting Felicia, but Thelma had been silent the entire time. All of Felicia's talent couldn't unglue Thelma's silent tongue.

But after that, in the house in Chicago, Carol had noted movements made by Thelma which could only have come from their visit to Ohio. They were Felicia's.

As Carol more easily called on Tim for help, he became comfortable enough that he coaxed her, "Read one chapter of my book and tell me what you think of it."

She replied with gentle earnestness, "Horror stories terrify me. I couldn't possibly. Just the occasional ticking on the windows is enough for my imagination."

"Ticking?"

"Yeah."

"I'll check it out. You should've told me."

Tim found and trimmed a couple of branches which might have been guilty with a cross-current wind. But he was disgruntled.

He had hoped Carol would read the smoldering love scene so that he could watch her reaction to it, but she did not. She had been an irritation from the time he first saw her.

Just about everyone Carol knew was at Tony's party. Even Tim. Since they were both going, they'd gone together. He was standing around in corners as he generally did. Carol figured he was working on plots. His absorption in his writing was similar to the quick small sketches she did when something especially caught her attention. And she could see that he'd take out a pad and pencil and make notes. He acted that way on occasion and everyone was used to him by now.

Actually, Tim was making notes for his book, but he was also keeping track of people and their conduct as a part of the job he'd been hired to do in watching over Carol.

It was the night of Tony's party when Carol ran into Megen Peabody again. They hadn't seen each other since their college graduation, and since there weren't any males there who caught their attentions, they were delighted to meet again.

Carol asked, "What are you up to?"

"The usual," Megen replied. "How about you?"

"I've been sketching baseball players from the TV, but they keep shifting the camera or giving us commercials or showing us unsuspecting guys doing something to their bodies or their noses or spitting. The catchers are couth because they lift the masks before they spit."

Megen agreed, "They are not inhibited, that's certain. But I find it charmingly basic and endearing. Why are you sketching from the TV?"

"My sketches and drawings of Cubs baseball players sell almost as fast as I finish them. People in Chicago are absolutely weird about baseball. I've never seen anything like it. They are so loyal! The Ohio teams are good and they play well, but the Chicago fans are very devoted."

Megen said brightly, "Let's go to a game! You can take stemmed opera glasses so that you can watch and sketch. And I can drool over one or two of the players and look around at the guys in the stands for something available."

"You're so subtle."

"I need someone to go along with me as cover. Why not you?"

Carol guessed, "You feel safe with me."

"Yeah. I've never known you to flirt or elbow your way between me and any guy. You've always been considerate."

"Tony said it's time for me to look around. I'm past twenty-four, you know." Carol laughed.

"Oh. Well. Just leave the ball players alone."

"Any particular one?"

Megen hesitated almost too long; then she declared lightly, "Anybody on the field."

"It seems rather selfish of you, Megen, to hog both teams." Carol chided.

"If I notice any particularly perfect man, I'll nudge you with my elbow. But you be quiet. Don't ask out loud, 'Him?' or 'What's his name?' or anything like that."

"I've never known you to be so shy about a man or men. Are you mooning over one…from afar? Tell me! That would make headlines in the sorority network."

"Go on, have your fun, get it out of your system. I've become tolerant as I've matured. You will find that you can also be tolerant." Megen smiled sweetly.

"Whoever it is you're watching, be sure you see him without his hat."

"Why?"

"I saw an Adonis. But then he took off his cap and he looked really strange. His face was too long, and his eyes were too close."

"You're picky."

"Well, Megen, I'm only twenty-four and not an ageing twenty-five like SOME I could mention."

"Yeah. So you know a player twenty-five is middle-aged for baseball. Just this spring, they brought a boy up from the minors—to the Show—who was…brace yourself…nineteen!"

"How rude. But I do have a foster brother, Saul, who is almost that age. He's a darling."

"A nice child."

"What show did they take the nineteen-year-old to see?"

Megen grinned. "Uh, you *are* a novice. The Show is the majors."

"Why do they call it that?"

"I haven't found out. It's probably just a name for playing in front of the crowds. I'd never even heard the expression until I saw the movie *Bull Durham*. Then I was half watching a game on TV in total boredom and heard the expression used. It caught my attention, and I saw this magic man. He's single, fortunately, so I don't have to ruin a wife's life by taking him away from her."

"Is this a little like film stars? What's the lure?"

"I think it's physical."

"Megen, with you, it's always been physical."

Megen stood up straight and looked around with a tiny smile on her face. "Yeah." Then her twinkling glance came back to Carol and she laughed.

Humor. That was what Megen had. It was the one thing that made Carol like her. Otherwise Megen was outrageous, but she saw herself and her circumstances with humor. And when Carol considered some of the past circumstances, it was just a good thing Megen had that trait.

During the party at Tony's, Carol heard a good many fine comments on her painting of Harlequin and Columbine. And she was pleased. The picture had been placed and lighted perfectly. It was a pleasure for Carol to see it there.

And it was a little sad. She hated selling her pictures. While she loved her paintings, how many could she keep?

Then, too, she had to eat. Ahhhh. Life's little realities. She sighed. Then she said to Megen, "What day is the game scheduled?"

"It's a night game on Wednesday. Bring a jacket, it can still be quite cool."

# Two

Since the two women were talking in competition with the noisy crowd at Tony's party, it didn't take any great talent for Tim to hear about Carol's Wednesday baseball commitment with Megen.

He did understand there was no danger of any kind for Carol in going to Wrigley Field to watch the Cubs. He was pleased she would go to the game. He did like baseball. And he was partial to the Cubs.

Carol and Megen's seats were about sixteen rows up and not quite to third base. Somebody Megen knew had season tickets and had given her the ones for that night. They were good seats. The two women settled in.

The excitement of the crowd was exhilarating. Why does one feel such a part of the Cubs' crowds? Along with almost everyone else, the two women bought hot dogs and peanuts and each recklessly had a beer.

Carol saw the shortstop almost immediately. "Look at that guy who's playing shortstop. I've used him as a subject for watercolors as I've watched the games on TV."

"Where?" Megen's voice was odd.

Carol didn't pick up on that. She just pointed. "Between second and third base."

"How'd you know that was shortstop?"

"I grew up with over a hundred other children, and we played ball in the back lot behind the barn."

"A *hundred?*"

"Give or take a few dozen."

"Yeah. Sure." Then Megen considered and asked, "A farm girl? I didn't know you were a farm girl."

"No. We had only ten acres and it was left unattended to go wild."

"—and a barn?"

"Yep."

Pensively, Megen mused, "I always wanted to be in a haystack."

"That sounds like the Megen I know and look at startled."

They watched the game. Since it was just the first part of the season, the players were a little pitched— uhhhh—hyper. Carol knew they would settle down. She watched the shortstop. Nothing he did was clumsy. He was an athlete. His movements were a joy to watch.

But Carol saw him as motion, as the essence of movement. He was so wonderfully coordinated. She would draw lines in the book on her lap. Although the book looked like any other book, it was full of blank pages. It was an artist's sketchbook. She could draw and not call attention to the fact.

If people think someone is observing them or sketching them, they quit picking their teeth and stand up straight and pull in their stomachs.

Some guys sitting a couple of rows in front of Carol and Megen would turn and observe them, and the two women were careful, looking away, looking through the flirtatious males, looking beyond or the other way. But the two women did draw glances. And after the April sundown, they bundled up. Even then, attention came their way.

Foul balls went into the stands, and it was interesting to Carol to see the adults scramble for the balls. The fans were really aggressive. And the winner who finally held aloft the retrieved ball was cocky and laughing. On one occasion, over off the corner of left field, the winner of the foul ball was a kid.

By the fifth inning, the score was four to three. The other team was ahead. The two novices in the sixteenth row were fully drawn into the excitement.

And it was the sixth inning when Megen's elbow poked Carol's side. Carol looked at her, but Megen was looking mesmerized toward the field. Carol looked around to see if someone was being unruly or out of bounds when Megen hissed, "Look at him."

Carol gave other discreet, quick glances around, and everyone appeared to be paying most of their attention to the field.

Megen ground out, "The pitcher."

So Carol lifted the glasses and looked. Then she stared because she couldn't think of anything positive to say. Nothing negative either, but he was just…a him.

She continued looking around, trying to think of something to say, and her glasses landed on the short-stop. He was standing with his feet apart and he removed his cap and wiped his face on his upper arm. She'd never seen him without his cap. He had red hair.

She thought it was a good idea for him to wear a cap. She'd never cared for red hair. He looked better with the cap on. He didn't wear any earrings or gold chains. That was different.

She made some more detailed sketches. He was lovely to draw.

The middle of the seventh inning came. Everyone stood up for the stretch and sang "Take me out to the ball game—" directed by Harry Carey. Along with the others around them, the two waved at the TV camera, which lingered on them. The whole crowd was jolly and laughing. It was fun.

They had another expensive hot dog and drank a costly soft drink.

Carol used the opera glasses and examined the crowd, the players and the umpires. One umpire insisted on laying his hand on the back of the catcher, for balance. Carol thought if she was the catcher, she'd turn around and swat the umpire one.

In the second half of the eighth, one pitcher laid a finger against one nostril and shot the other side clean. With all the real and acquired brothers she had, that was no surprise, but how could anyone with such a sweet name do something like that?

And the players were excited, that was obvious, but they were concentrating on the game. The score at the top of the ninth was tied.

The Cubs came up to bat at the bottom of the ninth. With two out and a man on base, the redheaded short-stop, Farthington, was the batter. A switch-hitter, he was batting left-handed, facing Carol. She was sketch-ing his excellent stance and how he held the bat at ready.

Then she simply watched him, her pencil idle.

He surely was a baseball player. She bet he'd settled on that when he was still quite young. He never made a jerky or awkward move. He was just faster and his movements were coordinated.

On the field, he spit, rubbed his nose on his sleeve and rearranged himself just like all the others. But he never noticed, really, that he did any of those things. His concentration was on the game.

Right then, he considered the runner who had stolen second. And he checked with the third-base coach for a long, serious look. The runner was now in position to make it home if the shortstop could hit a double.

He stepped back up to the plate with a call of three balls and two strikes. He wound up the bat in a series of swings and a little twirl at the top as he waited. The pitch was thrown, and he hit the ball with all his great might—the bat broke and the piece flew up into the stands. With those around watching the ball, the bat piece arced beautifully. Carol saw the batter's face really clearly as he turned to watch the bat piece in some dismay.

And the piece of bat came down and hit Carol's right thigh!

She said, "Ouch!"

Megen said, "Oh, my God! Did it break your leg?"

Carol replied, "I don't think so."

The roar of the crowd was terrific and almost drowned their words.

Several people around them asked, "You okay?" And two men wearing blue coveralls came to Carol. They were crowd control. They were concerned as they checked her thigh and fetched an ice pack to put on it. "There's a first-aid station under the stands, just behind home plate. Would you like to go there? Can you walk all right?''

Carol stood because everyone was standing and yelling. She could stand okay, and she assured the two, ''I'm sure it's fine. The bat was almost spent. The lap robe cushioned it.''

''We're sorry. Farthington will be concerned.''

She inquired, ''Farthington?''

''The batter. We need your name and address. We'd like you to see our doctor. You could go now if you like.''

''I'll be fine.'' She was positive.

''We'll want to hear from you. To be sure you're all right. You get a free ticket to tomorrow's game.''

She asked cautiously, ''Same seat?''

And they laughed.

She asked, ''What happened to the ball?''

''It went over the fence.''

''Which one?''

''The one in the middle.''

''It was a home run?''

''Yes!'' And he grinned.

''Well, then, the Cubs won!''

''Right!''

The two women smiled and shared the victory with the interested people around. Then they gathered their things and promised the crowd-control men to see a doctor about Carol's thigh, as they began to ease along the stairs and aisles to leave the ballpark.

So. His name was Farthington. That elite name had made no difference. He was not elegant.

But, golly, that guy could play ball.

So it was the next morning, and rather early, when Carol's doorbell rang. She moved her harmed leg slowly as she went over to peek through the viewer, and whom should she see but the shortstop!

She opened the door and just looked at him. He was beautiful. The moustache was untidy because it was curly, but his springy red hair was slicked down and his face was very serious. She said, "Well, hello!"

He replied, "I'm Ready."

She was cautious. "For what?"

"That's my name."

"Oh." She looked at him. "Come in."

He asked, "Are you okay?"

"Just fine. And you?"

"Your leg," he elaborated. "I found out it was you that got hit by my bat. I'm sorry."

"Did they make you come out here to apologize?" She stepped back and waited for him to come inside.

Like any male, he came in, looking around. "I coulda called, but I saw you."

"Oh." He had seen her clear up there in the stands? He had good eyesight.

He turned back toward her and asked, "How's your leg?"

She said with droll earnestness, "I'm going to have a spectacular bruise. It'll look a little like an orange you've forgotten in a bowl, and it'll be a sick orange color with the rather rotten purple of mold. Right now, it's just a strange red."

He watched her gravely. "Did you see our doctor?"

"No need." She lifted one hand and carelessly pushed the idea aside.

"You put ice on it?"

"Well, yes."

He said, "Let me see it."

"The ice?"

"Your thigh."

Her look then was more cautious. "I'm wearing slacks."

He blushed, and she was charmed.

She said, "I have some shorts I can put on. Take off your jacket and sit down. Just move the cats. They think they own this place."

She left the room, went down the hall into her room and closed her bedroom door. She skimmed out of her slacks and was stepping into her shorts when she heard: *Whap! Whap! Whap!*

He was killing the cats? She stared at the wall, quite wide-eyed, listening intently, and she heard him growl, "Why didn't you do it?"

Who? Do what? Someone else was there?

She put her slacks back on and, using the bedside table phone, she called her neighbor who was the writer. She whispered into the phone, "Tim, could you come down for just a few minutes?"

"You want something moved."

"No. It'll only be for a minute or so."

"Somebody's there?"

"Well, yes."

"He's giving you trouble?"

"He may have killed one of the cats."

"Oh? I'll come help him with the other one."

She considered the reality in which the choice in friends was always limited. She waited until she heard Tim's heavy footsteps down the stairs; then she exited her bedroom in time to hear the doorbell.

Straining the thigh, she walked more quickly than the thigh wanted to, as she went down the hall and into the living room/studio area. "Oh," she said brightly.

"Company!" She smiled a really big smile in the direction of a standing shortstop whose name was...Ready.

She opened the door and exclaimed in delight, "Tim! How *nice!* How's the book going?"

"Like always." He was very patient.

She turned brightly and said in a hostess way, "Uh...Ready, this is Tim Bolt. He's a writer and lives upstairs."

Ready nodded a couple of times, sober-faced.

Tim exclaimed, "Ready? Ready Farthington?" Then as people do with someone who is known, he told Ready, "Hey! You're the Cubs' shortstop!"

Tim moved over in long strides and wrung Ready's hand. "Man, what a game! You really whacked that ball. It's a good thing it was a home run. You just stood there. The bat went foul." Tim laughed. "But the ball went fair and over the fence. Did you see who got it? A woman— What're you doing here? You buy paintings?"

"No."

"Sit down." Tim was expansive. He moved the two cats—

Carol counted them. There were still two cats. What had Ready whapped?

—off the sofa in a rather rude way. "I never thought I'd actually meet you. Man, you can really play ball."

Ready still stood because Carol was standing and that was a part of manners. He looked at her. "I thought you were going to show me your thigh."

That made Tim blink. Then he got up very slowly and with quite a good deal of caution, as he eyed Ready. He asked, "Huh?"

Ready glanced at Tim and saw he was stressed for some reason. He said calmly, "My bat broke and it hit her thigh."

"Oh, was that you?" He looked at Carol as if she'd had a lucky experience being hit by a broken bat. "Did you get to keep it?"

"My thigh?"

Tim frowned his impatience. "The bat."

Ready moved and his breathing changed. "She was hurt."

Tim staked his territory. "We're neighbors, practically kin."

"Yeah?"

"Yeah."

Ready watched Tim for a minute in concentration; then he glanced at Carol. "May I see your leg?"

"I'll...go...put on my shorts."

Ready nodded. Tim sat back down, alert, a very careful participant in whatever.

As Carol went slowly into the hall, she heard Tim ask Ready, "Cubs going to win the pennant this year?"

Ready said, "Yeah."

"Good. I'll put money on it."

"Not too much. Not right away."

And Tim laughed.

She made short work of changing, but her thigh was being cranky, and she walked back down the hall a little more slowly.

"Here," said Ready. "Sit here." And he pulled out one of the high stools from beside one of her drawing tables. She sat on it and watched Ready. She gave Tim a glance to be sure he was still there.

Ready said, "I've had some experience with bruises. This one is worse than I thought it'd be. You really ought to see a doctor. You ought to have it X-rayed to be sure the bone is okay."

"I've been walking on it."

"People do that." Ready agreed, nodding. "After wrecks, after falls. It's best to be sure."

"All they'd do would be to wrap it."

"Well, they could give you some ultrasound treatments. That could help in the healing."

Tim said, "She's tough."

When Ready looked into Carol's eyes, she felt her eyes become unfocused. He took hold of her arm and said, "Steady."

Tim got up and came over to peer at her. "She is a little peaked."

"She should go to the doctor."

"I'll go along." Tim said that in a comforting way to Carol.

A little testy, she replied, "I'm fine."

But the two men paid her no attention at all. Tim got her jacket, and Ready waited, herding her. They went out to his car, and Tim was stopped in his tracks! He said, "My God! A Corvette! I never thought I'd ride in a car like that! Can I drive?"

Ready handed him the keys. Then he turned to Carol.

She wasn't impressed. Not because she was blasé. She just didn't care about cars. If it moved, it was a good car. This one had bucket seats and some god-awful little shelves in the jammed back. They were only for appearances. They were not meant to actually be used. She was frowning.

Softly, vulnerably Ready asked, "Don't you like it?"

"Tim, there's no—"

"Get in back." Tim looked at her in stark fear that she was going to keep him from driving the car.

And she thought of the irritated times he'd come clomping down the stairs to help her or to back her. She owed him. She gave him a sour look and said, "You drive. I'll sit in back."

He did not mistake her meaning. This was a full repayment and her books were cleared. After this, favors started fresh. He smiled.

Not too many people could manage to even attempt to get into such an impossibly limited area, but Carol was a contortionist. That is, she made it.

Tim turned the key and started the machine, and he made appreciative sounds. It drove like a hot knife through butter. He asked the owner, "How come you didn't get red?"

"The saleswoman said the red one clashed with my hair." He didn't say that with irony or with humor: he reported it.

Tim snorted, and the two men shared an amused glance. Then Ready added, "She decided yellow would seem cowardly and blue too passive. They didn't have a purple one, but they did have this green one on the lot, and I could drive it home. So I got green."

The men laughed as if that were very amusing. Carol listened to them and thought how cars bonded men. Cars and sports.

They went to see Ready's doctor. They were taken right into an examining room, and the doctor came, heartily welcoming. "So you're the one he hit. Man, he can really pick 'em!" He laughed cheerfully. He did the required testing and looked at the X-ray film before he said she was fine. "There're no broken bones, but it wouldn't hurt to put some cool cloths on the thigh."

She stretched her mouth into a smile and slid a look at Tim, who smiled like the Cheshire cat. Then she glanced at Ready, who was listening soberly.

Ready said he'd be with them in a minute. And he went to take care of the bill. Tim said, "I never thought I'd actually get to talk to one of the Cubs! God, Carol, thanks for calling me. I owe you."

She was surprised. He thought she had called so that he could meet a Cubs player? "I called you because—"

"I know," Tim said tenderly. "You feel you owe me for chaperoning you so much."

"No. I—"

"But I never thought you'd know a guy like Ready! He's really an okay guy."

"Tim. When I was in the bedroom changing into shorts, I heard—"

Ready came up and asked, "Okay?"

Carol said, "Uh—"

And Tim asked Ready, "May I drive back?"

Tim had said "May I." Carol looked at him in awe. "How'd you know those words?"

Being the man he was, he didn't misunderstand. She'd caught him being polite. He replied logically, "I'm a writer. I know all the words."

Ready watched them blankly and figured it was a private conversation. He again gave the keys to Tim, Carol again crawled skillfully into the back, and they returned to her apartment.

Ready accompanied her, and Tim tagged along. Inside her apartment, the cats were glad for company. Ready said, "We need to put some cool cloths on your thigh."

So she had to hunt some up.

Tim was on the sofa, Ready paced, and the cats watched. She had put a cloth under the faucet, gotten it wet and wrung it out. It was a damp, cool cloth as prescribed. She sat on a little rocker and put the cloth on her thigh. She'd done her share.

Ready squatted down by her, lifted the cloth and rearranged it. Remembering the *whap* sounds, his being that close made the skin on her back act up and her stomach was odd. She licked her lips.

He watched her do that as if he hadn't known people could.

She asked, "What did you kill while I was in the bedroom?"

Her eyes were so big and green. He'd never seen such beautiful green eyes before in all his life. Soberly he replied, "A mouse."

She said, "Oh."

Ready said, "One got away. Your cats didn't do anything."

"They weren't raised by a mouser."

He said, "I'll get you a mouser to teach them how it's done."

She demurred. "If you brought in another one, there would be three cats here."

"You could drown one."

"Good grief!"

"No?" He was so logical, solving her problems.

"Of course not!"

Ready stated it. "You're attached to them."

"Yes."

He nodded, assimilating that.

"Don't you like cats?"

"We just have barn cats. Mother won't allow them in the house."

"You're a farm boy?"

"Yeah."

"So'm I." She smiled.

He looked at her chest and doubted that.

"I mean I was raised on a farm. Almost one. We had a barn and a cow named Helen after mother's aunt. Aunt Helen wasn't amused. Mother said the cow had eyes just like her Aunt Helen's."

Ready watched her face, fascinated.

Tim asked, "Are you going to play today?"

"Yeah." He roused and looked at his watch. "I've got to go. I'll come back and see how you're getting along."

She nodded.

He stood up and walked out. Tim sat on the sofa musingly. He observed, "Two greats in one day. Met Ready and I drove his Corvette. I'm going down to the Grill and see who's there."

"Tim, it isn't even ten o'clock!"

"Somebody might be left over from last night." And Tim got up from the couch, walked across the room without another word and left.

Carol rose from the rocker to look for the dead mouse. It was in the wastebasket. How like a man. The thing would stink very soon. And there she was. She would have to do something about that nasty, dead little mouse.

She did do it. She took the tongs and carried the tiny body at arm's length away from her but high enough for the interested cats not to reach it, even jumping as they were, and she flushed the mouse.

She mentioned to the cats, "You've had every opportunity to eliminate the mouse problem on your own. I see no reason why someone should have to kill them for you."

One seal brown and the other cream colored, the cats listened politely, sitting neatly, with their tails around their paws. They blinked at her stupidity.

She spent the afternoon watching the Cubs on TV. Actually, she kept her gaze on the screen until she could see Ready. Ready? How'd he get such a name? She's never cared for redheads.

Then she saw him move and she was enthralled. She got up and went to her drawing board, got out some sheets of watercolor paper and began.

She had the clean water and dirty water bowls, she had the cloth to blot her brush; she pointed her brush in the time-honored manner of all watercolorists; she flicked the remaining water onto the floor; she went into another world.

As she stood by the table or sat on her high stool, time passed without attracting her attention, and she surfaced some long time later because her doorbell was ringing.

She got up and limped to the door, opened it and saw Ready standing there with violets in his hand. He stared at her, and she stared back.

He held out the flowers, and she smiled. She took the violets and said, "Thank you." She opened the door wider and said, "Come in."

"I have a cat."

"Oh?" She was cautious.

"My dad brought him up from the farm. He's a barn cat. It might not work, but he's a real good mouser and maybe he can teach those freeloaders how to catch mice before he goes back."

"He's on . . . loan?"

"Yeah. It made my dad very curious as to why I'd want Felix."

She muttered, "Felix, the cat."

Ready smiled. "My dad named him."

"Where . . . is Felix?"

"He's shredding a wooden fruit crate in my car."

"Uh, Ready, has this cat ever been in a house?"

"No. I don't think so."

She warned, "This could be a serious mistake."

"No, no. He's a mouser. You have mice. He'll be fine until they're all run off. Then he might be restless."

"You do know the cream-colored cat, Phoebe, is female?"

"He'll notice."

"The seal-brown cat, Caruso, is a male."

"Neutered."

"Yes. But he might be possessive."

Ready shook his head in a positive way. "He won't mind." But then curiosity got him and he asked, "Why did you name him Caruso?"

She replied the obvious: "He sings."

Ready bobbed his head in thoughtful, sober agreement.

Carol cautioned, "Phoebe is too young to be . . . molested by a barn cat."

Ready rubbed his face, took several steps and looked out a window at the darkening sky. "May I bring in Felix?"

"Can you control him?"

"He's just a cat."

That proved a lot right there. "Perhaps I should put my two in the bedroom."

"It'll be okay. Really." And he went outside just like any arrogant male who knows EVERYthing.

# Three

When Ready returned, bearing a rather shredded crate, Carol's green eyes widened and she opened her mouth to—

But the cat suddenly erupted out of the box into a red/orange, tiger-striped streak, and it was everywhere at once!

It was fascinating! Carol had never seen an animal move so quickly or see everything so fast. And he came back into the living room with a squirming mouse in his mouth!

The barn cat carried it over and laid it down in front of Phoebe, who was appalled! She jumped up onto the back of the sofa and spat something really degrading at the chewed-eared, raunchy invader.

Caruso was like a boy in his first pool hall that was also a bar. This was different, and the clientele was very different. He was so wide-eyed that he was all eyes.

"See?" asked Ready, indicating the cat. "He's being polite. He gave her a mouse."

With such patience that her mother would have gasped in admiration, Carol said through her teeth, "Phoebe doesn't like mice."

"Just watch." Ready was placidly confident.

Felix caught the mouse again and jumped up the two flights to the back of the sofa and again laid the mouse down by Phoebe, who hissed. Carol shrieked as the mouse disappeared behind the tacked pillows of the sofa back—

—and almost instantly Tim's heavy tread could be heard pounding down the stairs on the other side of the apartment wall.

Ready kept saying, "It's okay. Calm down. It'll just take a while."

Carol was about as wide-eyed as Caruso. Her voice was hollow. "It's in the sofa! The *mouse* is in the sofa!"

Tim was beating on the door. Felix was checking around the sofa in swift, efficient huntings. Phoebe had her back up, hissing, her tail was three times its normal size and she was absolutely outraged. But Caruso sat wide-eyed in amazed fascination.

Solving Carol's obvious distress, Ready went over to the sofa and thrust his hand down the various crevices allowed by the tacked pillows on the back and sides of the sofa. His face was earnest and logical. Felix followed, moving his head in jerks, watching quickly, seeing if the mouse would exit somewhere.

Carol fled to the rattling door and opened it, still looking back in horror toward the sofa. Tim came in, hyperventilating and gasping, "What happened? What's wrong? I've got to sit down."

"Not on the sofa!" Carol yelled the words.

Ready quickly said the same words, but he hadn't yelled, and he added, "We're looking for the mouse."

"You scared the hell out of me," Tim scolded Carol. "I think I'm going to faint."

Distractedly, Carol commanded, "Put your head down between your knees."

Tim gasped, "I can't do that."

"Try." She wasn't paying any real attention.

Tim inquired in a rather thin voice, "What in hell is going on?"

Enunciating, Carol said, "Ready's father brought their barn cat up here to teach Phoebe and Caruso how to catch mice." She was deadly serious and upset.

The meaning of the words soaked in, and Tim began to smile. He watched the two earnest hunters going through the crevices on the couch. He looked at Carol's indignation and her cats' agitation, and he laughed out loud. Then he became helpless with his laughter.

She was not amused.

Ready didn't even notice anything else. He was going to find that mouse for Carol and get it out of the sofa. Then Felix left the hunt to Ready and went off again. He wasn't gone five minutes when he came back *with another mouse!*

It was just too much.

Carol shrieked.

Felix did glance at her, but he was set on giving Phoebe a mouse. He went to her, but she fled. He followed.

Although Caruso's attention was on Ready, he looked, too, and the mouse ran out and across the floor! Caruso watched it go and looked back at the unaware, still-searching Ready. The man had not seen the mouse escape.

All was chaos.

Tim yelled, "There it goes!"

Ready got the broom and *Whap! Whap! Whapped!* the mouse.

Carol found herself standing up on her stool. Tim had entered the fray, and Phoebe came streaking in, followed closely by an intent Felix.

Carol yelled, "Get that cat out of here!"

Obediently, both Ready and Tim picked up a cat, but neither had the right one. Felix went off again and returned for the third time with a live mouse. He held it easily, standing under the limp Phoebe, who was looking down in some agitation.

Carol didn't blame her at all. Males are all so strange. There is simply no accounting for them. But—they're all females have. There's no alternative.

Quite avidly, Caruso was watching the mouse in Felix's mouth. He apparently hadn't thought of mice as participant entertainment before then. Caruso wiggled, and Tim absently let him go. Caruso went over and sat down to watch what Felix was going to do with the mouse.

Felix was bent on giving it to Phoebe. She did not want a mouse and stayed, hanging loosely from Ready's hand. Ready was trying to puzzle out Carol, who was acting rather unsettled.

Women were so interesting and so amazing, but their thinking was unfathomable. She was still standing up on that high stool, and she appeared a bit frazzled. It was probably her thigh. Maybe she hurt. It was just a little bruise, only about as big as an apple, but women did take on about little things. He asked her, "Does your thigh hurt?"

And she stared at him rather wildly and yelled, "My thigh? My *thigh!* Good Lord!"

And Ready looked off to one side and tried to sort out what she might mean by that.

Felix glanced over at the fascinated Caruso, bit through the mouse's neck and laid the dead mouse aside. Then Felix jumped up on the table near to Ready and said, "Meour" in a directing way.

Ready looked at the barn cat and thought he really looked pretty scruffy. Maybe they should have taken him to a vet and gotten him cleaned up. Naw. The damned cat would have wrecked the vet's whole place.

But his dad could have thrown Felix into the cattle trough. That would have been a good idea. Then Felix could have spent the two hours it took to get from the farm to Chicago licking his fur and getting it neat and orderly. And the crate would have survived the shredding.

Too late for that.

Caruso reached out a paw and nudged the dead mouse. It didn't move. He looked up at Felix and gave a brief, inquiring meow.

The country bumpkin gave Caruso a cold glance and said, "Meourrr," with three *r*'s.

Caruso looked back at the mouse and then went over and sniffed it. He batted it again. Then he picked it up in his mouth...and the body and tail hit against his chest. He tried to look down to see what was hitting him and his forehead wrinkled.

Felix said, "Meourrrrr" in an impatient, superior, irritated manner and five *r*'s.

Caruso held still; then he flipped his head and let go of the mouse. It fell at some distance. Caruso the Hunter leaped into the air and stood on his back feet like a sparring partner, shadow boxing; then he fell on the mouse and "killed" it. It was dead.

Caruso sat like a sacred Egyptian cat, smooth and perfect, and he blinked his yellow eyes smugly.

Felix dropped effortlessly off the table and said something silently to Caruso. Then Felix went off. Caruso watched alertly and he hesitated, but he did follow.

Curiosity and cats are linked. Phoebe wiggled and said something unladylike to Ready, who put her down. But as he moved his hand to smooth her fur, she avoided him and trotted off after the two males.

Tim went over and put his hands up to lift Carol down from the stool, but Ready said, "I'll do that."

Tim was somewhat surprised. He hesitated, as if to challenge, but he blinked and backed off.

Ready went over to Carol and looked up at her. It was a strange encounter. They'd only just met, but the two were very conscious of each other. She as an artist. He as a male.

Carol was standing on the thirty-inches-high stool, and Ready stood below her. His head was just about even with her ribs. He looked up at her as a redheaded, moustached Romeo might have looked up at a streaked-blonde, green-eyed Juliet.

He put his hands on her waist and held her a minute. She didn't resist or protest. She noted his eyebrows were as undisciplined as his hair and moustache. And the hairs were not all the same color.

She leaned a little and put her hands on his shoulders. Effortlessly he lifted her down...very, very slowly. He never broke eye contact. And his muscles didn't even tremble, nor did his breathing change in that show-offy manipulation.

He pulled his elbows back, still holding her, and set her feet right in front of his. He did that without bending over. The only touching parts were his hands on her waist and hers still on his shoulders.

She blinked, finally, and was aware of the strength he'd just flaunted so beautifully. She said, "You're so strong." She did. She actually said that and she didn't even blush. She was wide-eyed and impressed.

He didn't reply. His breathing picked up a little and his face was so serious that his eyes looked naked.

Agitated, alarmed, Tim cleared his throat.

The distracted pair looked at him in a vague way, as if they had been expected to do that... and did.

Tim was very earnest and frowned. He'd lived upstairs from Carol for some months now, acting as her protector. He'd thought... He said, "Uh..."

What does a man say to a Cubs shortstop who can lift a woman off a high stool that way? Tim asked, "Have you had supper?" He looked at Carol.

She turned her head and looked outside rather vaguely. "What time is it?"

"Almost seven." He glanced at Ready rather superiorly and explained in a knowledgeable manner to show how well he knew Carol, "When she paints, she forgets the time."

She exclaimed, "I missed lunch!"

Tim moved a little more freely and gave Ready the information, "I have to remind her to eat."

Ready gazed at her. "I haven't eaten, either. Want to go out?"

With Ready's shutout words, Tim was back in the blizzard of isolation. He said, "I have—"

But she was still studying Ready. She said, "I have a frozen pizza."

Tim added hastily, "I have a salad."

Ready just looked down at Carol and told her, "I have some red wine in the car. A fan gave it to me after that home run when the bat hit you. You ought to share the wine."

"I'll go get the salad." Tim started for the door.

The two glanced over at the departing Tim. Carol said, "G'bye."

"I'll be back—with the salad." He stressed that.

She said a vague "Okay."

Tim left the door open. He didn't want to come back and have to knock. She might not open it again.

Ready was still holding her waist, therefore she had to tilt her head back to look up into his face. As if the door problem had communicated to him, Ready asked, "If I go out that door, will you let me back in?"

It seemed an odd question. Did it have more meaning? She didn't know. She was as serious as he when she replied, "Um-hmmm," and additionally, she nodded very slightly, but she sustained her blank expression.

He moved his hands a little on her waist, as if he weren't aware of how he could release her and he was testing for an exit. Or...he might have been seeing if she had any fat roll above her waistband. She stood a little straighter, but she didn't step back.

"Your eyes are green."

She didn't exclaim, "Really?" And she didn't go over to a mirror and check that out, she replied, "Yours are blue."

His face was still very serious. He asked, "How's your thigh?"

"Okay."

"Let me see."

With a prissy tilt of her head, she said, "I'm not dressed for viewing. It's okay."

"You've been keeping the ice on it? Does it hurt?"

"Cold cloths. And I have a pill or two."

"I'm sorry."

"Well, if you didn't want the bat to break, you could put a steel rod down it."

"Illegal."

"You've tried?"

He shook his head, still looking at her, his hands still doing those caressing little half-inch movements on her waist. Movements that hardly moved.

But she was intensely aware that his hands were on her waist. She ought to back away. She didn't know him well enough to stand that close to him. She'd never particularly liked redheads. They didn't tan at all well. He was gently tanned. He didn't have any freckles. His eyelashes were pale and thick.

Tim thundered down the stairs on the other side of her wall and came through the still-open door. He was carrying the salad in a bowl. He stopped dead, staring. He was shocked because they hadn't moved.

The pair turned only their heads and looked at Tim inquiringly.

Tim knew they had completely forgotten him, supper, time, everything. He was stunned. Was this one of those cosmic things writers wrote about? He was a writer, he knew, he knew. How could he counter the shocking distraction that had hit his staked-out woman?

He'd been so clever and careful and sneaky. He had willingly filled the role of protector until her dependence on him could get her attention. He'd made no threatening moves; he'd done everything by his own scenario. What had gone wrong?

He still had access.

He went past them into the kitchen. He began to take the plates down. Then he looked in the freezer for the pizza. She had strange things in the freezer—like wax pencils—but, naturally, there were no mice.

Tim knew that Carol used none of the lower cabinets, except for big, quickly washable pans. Everything else was in the mouse-safe upper cabinets. She vacuumed everything every day. The mice probably visited her apartment only to experience cleanliness, not to find food.

Ready went out to his car for the wine, and Tim resisted barricading the door against his return. How could he tell a woman who couldn't remember to eat that a Cubs shortstop as competition was unfair?

Tim came back with a case, and in it were seven bottles of red wine.

One pizza was not enough. Carol opened two boxes of Kraft's Italian Spaghetti and enhanced it to Liza's Original Kraft's Italian Spaghetti qualifications. That meant adding parsley, black olives, hamburger and onions—

And, of course, she heated French bread gently imbued with American garlic butter. With that, they would have Tim's Chicago salad and Ready's French wine. A nice Italian meal.

Tim had suggested one bottle be opened so that the wine could breathe. It was a red wine, a Bordeaux 1978 from CHATEAU BEYCHEVELLE.

Tim blinked. He'd researched wine for a book and he knew that brand ran close to seventy bucks a bottle. He picked up one of the bottles and read the label to be sure. Then he said, "I have a gallon bottle of last year's Chablis. I'll go get that. This wine should be drunk at a perfect place with the perfect person of the opposite gender, overlooking the ocean at sundown."

Ready commented, "I'm a beer man, myself."

Tim thought sadly, no soul.

Carol smiled at Ready. "I'm a beer drinker, too."

Ready grinned. "What?"

"Bud."

"Right!" He held up his palm just over his head, and she put hers to it in the brief greeting/agreeing/celebrating shared clap.

Tim realized that neither of them had souls. He felt his eyes prickle at the thought of them guzzling down that wine with spaghetti and garlic and never savoring the essence of it. They probably didn't even sniff the bouquet or roll the wine on their tongues. Again Tim said, "I'll get the Chablis."

"No." Ready delayed Tim. "Help me use this up."

Help him…use…it…up. Mentally Tim put his hand to his head.

Carol opened out a gate-legged table and covered it with a cloth from a high shelf. The two men sat down at the table, and she served. She filled their plates, and Ready poured wine into the glasses.

He lifted his glass and said, "A toast." The other two lifted their glasses, and Ready toasted: "The pennant!"

Carol said, "Hear, hear!"

Tim nodded and sipped the ambrosia. And it was superb.

After a second thoughtful sip, Tim said, "I'll trade you a case of Bud for one of the bottles."

And Ready grinned. "Done!" Then he added, "I gave my dad a couple of the bottles for bringing Felix up here today."

"Where does he live?" Carol asked.

"On our farm in the southern part of Porter County over in Indiana."

Carol chided. "That was an imposition to come all that way just to bring a cat here."

"It's only a couple of hours away. The cat was a nuisance. He doesn't like riding in cars. He relates cars with visits to the vet, you understand."

Carol understood. "My cats are like that."

Ready explained, "My family comes up for most of the games. They came for the game today. So it wasn't a special trip." He smiled a little because his mother, particularly, had been avidly curious as to why he wanted a barn cat for a visit.

Carol said kindly, "They must be very proud of you."

Ready looked benign. "They like all their kids."

"How many are there?" she inquired respectfully.

"Four."

She scoffed, "Is that all?" And she laughed.

"Okay." He put down his fork and waited. "How many?"

She tilted her head in a top-lofty manner and replied, "I think it was twenty-seven or twenty-eight, last count."

"What?" He was unbelieving.

She lifted her brows and gestured with one hand, turning it out to indicate openness. "Kids. The actual, foster and adopted." She explained that in an aside. "We're not counting, here, those who just sheltered for a while." Then she grinned. "You've never seen such a press of people as we have on holidays or at weddings. And the kids' kids! It's bedlam."

An only child, an orphan, Tim felt something of a shudder along his back over the idea of all that crowd.

But Ready laughed and his attitude became a little competitive. "Well now, we do have relatives around and about Porter and down into Jasper County, in Pulaski County to the east and even farther over in Kosciusko County."

"I hate a braggart." She leaned back in her chair, sighed and looked bored.

He pulled a chunk of bread from the last loaf and commented, "I guess the only thing I can do is take you around and introduce you to all of them so you can believe me."

And she countered, "Only if you agree to going to Temple, Ohio, on a holiday." She stressed the last three words.

"I'll take it into consideration."

She replied, "How kind of you."

But Tim became alarmed. They were talking about traveling together! He said, "I'll go along with a counter and keep score."

And Ready replied, "That's a good idea, Tim. I've got one of those."

Tim said seriously, "But how can she be sure you don't cheat and add a couple each time?"

"I'm a simple, honest man."

Carol and Tim both laughed. But as sly as Ready's words sounded, they were true. That was exactly how he saw himself. He'd never had a reason to be sly. Not like some.

The talk then was of baseball. Carol questioned, and Ready explained. They were very animated, and Carol became flush-faced and sassy.

Tim felt like an unneeded/unwanted chaperon. He felt a little nostalgia for pre-Ready days. He looked at Carol, feeling very much like a homeless dog in the snow, staring through a window at a holiday gathering. He was staunch. He didn't whimper. Not out loud.

With their supper finished. They moved rather sluggishly, clearing the table. Ready helped in that. Tim, however, emptied their wineglasses into his and drained the last drops from the bottle. He then lifted the glass to view the last jewel drops against the light.

Carol inquired, "Have you developed a drinking problem?"

"Not wine. Wine is for artists. Writers drink the hard stuff."

"I hadn't known that," she scoffed.

"It's a rule." Tim felt she was trying to pick a fight. She never had before then. She was a courteous woman. He frowned at her. Was she trying to quarrel so that he'd storm out of her apartment, leaving Ready alone there with her...and...ready? Tim decided he wouldn't budge.

They made short work of the cleanup. Carol vacuumed again to be sure there were no tasty crumbs on the floor.

Ready wandered over to see her studio. There were her pictures of a redheaded baseball player. Him. He was stunned.

"That's you." She had no hesitation or embarrassment in telling him that, but she said it ordinarily. She didn't blush or squirm or simper.

Tim noted that because he watched her.

"This is great!" Ready held one up of him batting. "You've got that added body effort just right. You can really draw!" He beamed at her.

She had her masters in the fine arts.

She showed him other watercolors she had done of baseball players, and she watched his amazement. They were "caught" pictures. One was a stretched-out throw of a ball from deep left field that would have to've made home plate. Another was the stretch to catch one that was just a little high. And one was of the batter. They were simply superb.

"You have a nice little talent." Ready beamed at her.

And she said, "So do you."

Ready didn't inquire what that might be. He said, "I can play ball."

"Most assuredly. You're a pleasure to watch."

And he looked at her. He looked in a very quick glance down her and even more quickly back to her face, and he blushed scarlet but said nothing.

She'd never had such a charming compliment.

Tim stood, shifting from one foot to the other, trying not to call attention to himself and be booted out of her place, but he needed to distract her from any man who gave her tongue-tied compliments. He cleared his throat.

Both looked at Tim and waited for him to speak. He said, "Carol's a great artist."

She smiled just a little, amused.

Ready asked her, "Do you sell your pictures?"

"Sometimes."

"I'd like to have this one."

"I'll give it to you for paying my doctor bill."

"I had to do it. I was the one that hurt you."

"I've done about a dozen watercolors of you, and I've sold six or seven. With the games on TV, you've been my model, and I haven't given you a model's fee."

"You gave me supper."

"You supplied the wine."

"It was free."

"And you brought Felix— Where're the cats?"

And they all looked at the still-open apartment door.

The cats were gone.

# Four

The three went out of Carol's apartment, into the big entrance hall. In a worried voice, Carol felt the need to mention, "The cats have never been outside except in their carriers or in the car. They won't understand cars and streets or—"

Ready dismissed that. "The front door is closed and locked."

"If it was, how did you get back inside?"

"Right. It was open while I was out getting the wine."

She was concerned. "They'll be terrified."

Ready soothed, "We can't be sure they went outsi—"

She looked up the empty stairs as she interrupted, "Felix would have shot out of this house like a...shot. And my two would have gone along like the trusting lambs they are."

"They're cats," Ready clarified. "They'll be okay. They have nine lives."

She gasped at the very idea of the cats losing any of the nine. "And they're being led around by that hooligan, Felix!"

A bit impatient, Ready assured her, "He's a good, sensible barn cat. He'd weigh the chances. He's inside the house somewhere. I'll look."

There was a rude "merrrorah" from the utility closet at the bottom of the stairs. That's when they noticed the *row* of mice lined up along one wall. One mouse was a pinto.

Carol exclaimed, "They're in the closet?"

"Mine is, at any rate. Here." He opened the door. "Felix?" Someone had apparently closed the closet door.

Felix came out in something of a temper. He put another mouse in the line and hissed at them. Then he went back into the closet.

"Where's Phoebe?" She tried to see inside the dark closet. "Caruso?"

And there was a scrambling at the back of the closet.

Well, a woman who has seen a line of dead mice nearby, isn't going to hang around in a dark closet and see what any strange sounds might be. Carol shot out of the closet similarly to the way Felix had done. However, Felix had willingly gone back inside. Carol did not.

All was silent.

Ready whistled the way one did when calling a dog, and he said, "Okay, Felix. Come here." That only proved he was a strange man, the kind who would think a barn cat was civilized.

Tim said, "Get me a flashlight, and I'll look."

Carol did that and, returning, carefully closed her apartment door. One of those laid-out mice might not be dead—enough. She gave the flashlight to Tim. It was humongous. Only the Coast Guard and women had flashlights like that. He turned it on and watched the beam and shone the light around in some wonder.

Carol wasn't patient. She said, "Phoebe may be out-side."

Ready dismissed that. "She's in the basement."

"Now . . . how would she get down there?"

"There's some kind of hole in the back of the closet. Can you hear any of the cats? It's just the kind of thing Felix would find and introduce to your cats who haven't ever had any kind of adventure. They must be having a good time. Look at all those mice lined up along the wall."

Carol glanced quickly. "We had a calico cat named Calico who did that. She put the field mice by our front door. We figured she was just showing us that she was devoted to her duty. She basked in praise."

From the inside of the closet, Tim said, "You're right, Ready. There's a hole here. The light stops at a turn, but the slant of it appears to go to the basement. Here comes Caruso . . . and he's got a mouse!"

It turned into a very interesting evening. The three went knocking on apartment doors and invited the inhabitants down to see the spoils of mouse war. And they decided if the cats were that involved, they'd give them more room and they all opened their doors.

Having done that, the humans reassembled and left the cats to their adventure. They went into Carol's apartment where Ready opened the rest of the wine bottles. And everyone savored and discussed the different taste.

Tim did save his one reserved bottle. "I'll get you the case of beer next week."

"Naw. Enjoy the wine." And Ready clapped him on the shoulder in a friendly way.

Tim gave some fleeting thought of regret that he and Ready were doomed to be enemies. Their battle over Carol would be to the death of friendship. He wondered if Ready knew he had competition—that Tim Bolt was staunchly in competition for Carol's regard?

Without a game the next day, Ready was lax and easy, staying around. Tim said, "I thought athletes had to be in bed by ten."

And Ready gave the stock reply without even thinking about it: "Whose?"

Tim forced a faint smile on his sick green face as his jealousy grew.

Carol's guests exclaimed and argued over the baseball watercolors she'd done, and they propped them up to see better.

Hastily Carol said, "Let me," in a no-nonsense voice as she took the sheets from sturdy fingers.

She put a large eight-by-ten-foot cardboard against the front of cabinets and pinned the sheets to the board. She arranged the sheets for an overall balance. The brown of that background was complementary to the white sheets of paper and the reds and tans and stripes of the figure depicted, Ready Farthington.

"Hey!" said one of the grad students. "You're *that* Ready Farthington!"

"Yeah." Ready smiled. He didn't say, Well, I'll be darned! or I wonder if my dad knows?

And they all discussed baseball and told Ready how to win games and what the other players should be doing.

Ready was really very adult and kind about their advise.

The poet went off to one drawing table and took paper and a pencil from Carol's stock and began to write a poem.

The stockbroker was a little ticked until he realized it was about the barn cat's visit to the Big City.

Here and there during the evening, Tim checked on the mouse accumulation.

It was late when they heard a scramble in the hall. They went to the door cautiously. Apparently Phoebe had brought up a live mouse and hadn't given it the coup de grace. She flopped down on her side, exhausted, and allowed Felix to sunder the mouse.

Felix looked over to Phoebe, and she moved her head on the floor so that her chin was up; then she looked at the raunchy cat. He went over to her and licked her nose. She touched him gently with one paw.

Carol was owl-eyed. How had her house cat learned those kind of motions in just one day? Why... Phoebe was a flirt!

Caruso nose-counted the line. He sat down very smug and a part of the adventure.

Tim suggested, "Go upstairs and see if you can find any in my place."

And the others said similar things.

Felix had listened to the requests and looked at Ready. Ready waved an arm to indicate the stairs. He said, "So... We don't have a hole for you. Try the stairs."

Felix looked at Phoebe. She laid her head back on the floor and curled her tail in one slow movement of acknowledgment. She stayed put.

Felix gave a three-*r*'d meow to Caruso and headed up the stairs.

Admiringly, Ready said, "You just can't beat a barn cat for stamina."

Carol shivered. "At least Phoebe and Caruso aren't eating the nasty things."

And it was Tim who put in the ringer: "They don't overeat."

Carol gagged.

The men all laughed. Even the poet. How could a poet laugh at something so awful?

She said to Thelma, "Men."

And Thelma replied, "God love 'em all."

"You just wonder what women did to have to cope with them as punishment."

That started a great debate. They overwhelmed Carol, and she wasn't really overwhelmable. She was staunch and steady and a damned good arguer because she'd been raised with so many siblings who had never been neutral on ANY subject at all! Carol wasn't overwhelmed by logic, she was overwhelmed by voice volume. Males have heavy voices.

Consider the tiny mew that Phoebe used and the meow with a varying number of *r*'s that barn cat used.

But just after midnight, Carol was getting a little hoarse, and Tim suggested that they concede the argument since she was getting hoarse.

In a hoarse voice, she denied that.

The men all laughed, and it really ticked Carol to be treated like a pet to be indulged.

After they'd all left, Tim last of all, Carol got ready for bed. All three cats were on her bed, licking and licking and licking, and that rather revolted Carol be-

cause she knew what they'd been doing all evening ...
primarily.

As she gargled her hoarse throat, she continued her
arguments in her head and all the nuances she discovered were absolutely brilliant. Unfortunately she was
too tired to write them down.

Since he had no game that next day, Ready was there
for breakfast. Carol had things she had to do. She was
just doing the preliminary gestures of rejection with her
hands, when Tim showed up with his coffeepot.

Carol was in her Japanese kimono that Felicia had
given her because it went with her coloring and because it was such a feminine garment. A change. Carol
stood around as the men greeted each other in a stiff-
legged way, and then they went into the kitchen to start
breakfast.

It is very irritating when people have no inkling that
they are intruding. She said, "I don't want eggs and
bacon."

Ready said, "Naw. We're having my mom's pan-
cakes. I know how to make them just right."

Salty could cook. There was the off chance that
Ready could, too. She went in and showered and
dressed in jeans, a shirt and tennies. Her thigh was an
interesting color of a storm cloud ... that mottled dangerous dark blue. She stared at it thoughtfully and went
to her drawing table.

Tim came to her with food and said, "Eat."

He put some things on the table next to the one where
she was working, and she chose from the selection now
and then along the way, but she was lost in the work
before her.

The watercolor was a storm at sea. The blues and
greens and tearing foam with a boat in peril. It was

dramatic, and seeing it, the winds were on the viewer's face and streaming through his hair and it made him shiver.

At her elbow, Ready said, "I'd like you to do a picture of our barn."

"The...barn?"

"Yeah. It's a real farm barn. It isn't a showplace. It's a real one."

"I'd be delighted. I can do that when you take Felix back."

"Have you noticed that he's settled in?"

"I can't have three cats."

"If he keeps at her that way, you'll have more than three."

"What?"

"Don't you know they're in love?"

"Good gravy. Get him out of here!"

"Too late."

"Ready..."

He grinned. "Yeah!"

And her doorbell rang.

Tim went to the speaker just as if he were at home there. He didn't want Ready doing it, so he did. He punched the button and said, "Yeah?"

"Sorry."

"Hey! This is...Carol's."

"Oh, Tim! It's Megen."

"I knew your voice. We met at Tony's. Remember?"

"I'll...uh...come back another time."

"Come on in." He pressed the release.

Megen came to the door and it was already opened by Tim. She said, "I didn't mean to intrude."

"Thanks for the vote of confidence. It's misplaced . . . so far."

"Oh." Megen came inside, glancing around because she hadn't been there since Carol moved in. Megen was animated and restless as always...until Ready stood up.

Carol said, "Well, hello! What brings you out this early?"

Megen didn't hear anything. She stared. She went immobile and just stared. The hyperagitated Megen was absolutely still. Incredible.

Ready smiled a little and moved more slowly. He blinked and narrowed his eyes a bit.

Megen just stared. Her lips were parted.

Carol asked, "Have you had breakfast? We're just finishing."

Tim said, "She's just finishing. Ready and I've been finished for over an hour or more."

Megen heard nothing. She stared.

Carol said, "Megen, this is Ready Farthington."

Megen said, "Yes."

"Ready," Carol continued, "this is Megen Peabody."

"Hi."

Carol continued, "Megen's the one responsible for your bat hitting my thigh."

Ready raised his eyebrows politely, blinking a couple of times and said, "Mmmm," as people did with Carol's rather enigmatic sayings.

Carol elaborated, "She made me go to the ball game because she I—"

Megen intruded. "I like baseball."

"Most women come to see the players." Ready grinned at Megen.

Megen said, "I like the game."

Ready said readily, "Whatever game you'd like, you'd attract men to it."

Carol smiled and said, "Hear, hear! A silver tongue."

Megen's heart sank. How confident Carol was to tease in that way.

And Tim's soul groaned.

Ready said, "If you like it that much, why don't you girls come out to L.A. and give the Cubs some support? You could spend the weekend there."

Carol smiled at Megen and asked, "Are you game?"

"I've always wanted to see ... L.A."

Carol said, "Felicia has commented about actually standing at the corner of Hollywood and Vine when she was sixteen. And she walked on the sidewalk that has the stars' names. You could take a picture of me doing that. It would make her smile."

So Tim called Salty and said, "Next weekend, she and Megen are going to L.A. to see the Cubs play out there. Uh. I guess I should go along. I said I would."

"Get a suite at the Biltmore. Take them around and show them the sights. I'll send the cash to the hotel."

"Naw," Tim declined. "We'll do it careful. I've made reservations at the Holiday."

"Pay attention. It's wild out there."

"It's no worse than Chicago."

"California is different." Salty warned. "You have to know that. You've been out there."

"Well ... yeah. You got to have an open mind."

"My mind is parentally closed."

"Geez." Tim snorted.

"Yeah. Take care of her, Tim."

"You gotta know I'll do that. Megen, too, since Carol'll be with her."

"How do you like this anvil I hung around your neck?"

"She's something special," Tim's voice was tender. "And she's a great artist. I watch her work, and she makes my hair stand on end."

"It's the new style for men."

"You got your hair like that?"

"In . . . Temple . . . OHIO? You jest."

"You're just bragging because you still *have* hair. I hate a bragging man."

"I still have it because Felicia tried to pull it out so many times that the roots strengthened with the exercise."

And Tim laughed.

He hadn't laughed much lately. He'd lost a little weight and he felt that his life might not go the way he wanted it to go. He sighed and said, "I'll be in touch."

"Hang in there."

"Yeah." He hung up gently, wondering just exactly what Salty meant by that. Did Salty doubt that he could take care of Carol? God. He wanted to spend his *life* taking care of Carol.

With the team, Ready had flown out to L.A. right after the last game at Wrigley Field on Wednesday night. The first game wasn't until Friday. They had Thursday off to rest and adjust to the two-hour time change. A lot of the ball players played golf.

But Tim, Carol and Megen didn't fly out to L.A. until Friday. Tim sat at the window and was pensive. He was taking Carol halfway across the country to see another man. She would watch a man who played ball like every man dreams of playing. Ready Farthington was the perfect athlete, and he, Timothy Bolt, was taking his woman out to watch that man. How ironic.

So they got there just in time for the game.

L.A. won.

"Tomorrow. We win tomorrow." Ready was confidently sure.

The only good thing about the weekend was that Ready didn't have a whole lot of time with them. It was Tim who took the two women out and about and showed them the town, Hollywood, the movie stars' sidewalk stars, and they went to see the sidewalk squares that held impressions of stars' signatures over those of their hands and feet in cement mementos.

The visitors saw Ready a little on Friday night and some on Saturday and Sunday around the games. The Cubs won the last two games.

As much as Tim had tried to keep the four together, Ready did get Carol away once. Not for long, but long enough to make Tim sweat.

Megen spent the time in a blue funk. She was so sunk that she was no help at all. A zombie. She irritated the hell out of Tim. Did she think she was the only one suffering?

Tim felt he'd lost all hope. He'd watched as Ready had kissed Carol goodbye, but it hadn't looked like a goodbye kiss to him.

Ready had been holding Carol to him. Close up. The whole length of them. The kiss had been consuming and erotic and blasted the smog film off the buildings all around the area. Tim felt the rejection of the electric kiss all through his body, but it wilted his soul.

Still stunned by what he'd witnessed, he'd watched as Ready slowly released Carol. Then a shocked Tim saw Megen give Ready a kiss! That had surprised the shortstop who had stared after Megen. Tim surmised that Megen had offended Ready with her boldness. After the kiss that Ready had shared with Carol. Tim knew Ready wouldn't have wanted another woman's mouth on his.

All the way back to Chicago, sitting in a row on the plane, all three had been silent. Tim knew that Carol was dreaming of Ready, that Megen had a king-size crush on Ready, and he—Timothy Bolt—was the odd man out.

It rained in Chicago the next morning. Tim lay in his big, lonely bed and was discouraged. He didn't know if he wanted to get up or just stay in bed and forget the world. So, of course, he rolled out, put on jogging clothes and went out into the cold, sloppy rain.

He ran and ran and ran, but his thoughts kept up. He finally went back to the big old house and into the front hall. Carol's door was open. That was the house invitation to visit.

He was sweat-and-rain soggy; but, wanting to see her, he forgot that as he went hesitantly into her apartment.

She was sitting on her stool, her elbow on her drawing table, her chin propped on her hand. She was staring out the long windows at the rain.

"What's the matter?"

She didn't turn or greet Tim. She sighed in great melancholy.

So Tim asked tensely, "What's wrong?"

She replied hollowly, "Ready kissed me."

Tim went rigid. Ready had sneaked her away from his protection that one time. "Did he— Did he—"

A little irritated, she snapped. "I just told you that he did." There was a pithy silence. "It was very pleasant."

"Did he touch you?"

She was impatient and gave Tim an exasperated scowl. "If he kissed me, he *had* to've touched me."

There was silence. Tim didn't know how to continue. Why was she so cross?

He moved cautiously, slowly, breathing roughly. He sounded a little like an air conditioner that needed the filter cleaned out, his breathing was laboring so.

She sighed as if in despair.

Tim closed his eyes against asking it, but he had to know. "What'd he do?"

"I *told* you that he kissed me!" she said shortly. Then she added with trembly melancholy, "The sky didn't fall in." She turned great, tragic Felicia eyes toward the foggy, soggy day and was silent.

He was stunned. A Cubs shortstop had kissed her, and the sky hadn't fallen in. He moved like any male cat with a female. He hardly moved at all and when she looked at him, he went absolutely still.

As the silence stretched and stretched, she volunteered faintly, "I was disappointed."

"You want the sky to fall in?"

"I expected it."

He didn't know what to do. He should kiss her. If she was really waiting for something to happen, he would be willing to try for that happening with her. A man who is almost thirty knows that when a woman has been temporarily disappointed with one man, she might be willing to taste another man just to compare them. She needed to be kissed by another man. But he'd been jogging and he not only was soggy, he didn't smell that great.

He said, "I have to shower." And the idea of running up those stairs and showering and getting back down and kissing Carol made his voice hoarse.

She replied, "You're probably catching cold from being out in this fog and running around practically naked."

He looked down quickly and saw that his wet, faded shorts were almost transparent...and revealing. He was jolted. He turned swiftly and said, "I'll be right back."

She slid a hooded-eyed glance at him and didn't reply.

Tim ran from her apartment. He went up the stairs two at a time. He went into his apartment and closed the door. He would have given anything to have had a long mirror so that he could have checked what she'd seen with her sloe-eyed glance, and how she'd seen it and if she'd been shocked or afraid of him.

He went into the bathroom and stripped. He showered and put on a scentless deodorant and dressed. He was quick. Then he took off his shirt and shaved very carefully, feeling for every whisker.

And he went downstairs with trembly anticipation and a condom in his pocket. Her door was closed.

Tim hesitated. Then he knocked gently. He was proud of himself. He wanted to kick in the door, but he only knocked gently.

She called, "Come in."

He would, he would. He opened the door and stepped inside, standing straight, powerful and male. He glanced quickly to see her, and there she stood in her studio with a fussy woman holding a nasty little pug dog, and a skinny man with a tiny moustache and big yellow teeth.

Had Tim been a balloon, he would have deflated. As it was, he simply stood there in something like shock. And he instantly felt a great and unsupportable distaste for the couple with Carol.

Carol asked politely, "Is there something you need?"

Oh, yes. "I'll come back later."

Coolly she replied, "I have appointments today. Perhaps another time."

She was piqued. He smiled as he would for a dog that showed its teeth and was snarling. He replied gently, "Perhaps tomorrow." And he matched not only her wordage, but her tone.

She lifted her chin and gave him a look that said touché. But the look was hostile.

As any man almost thirty has learned to do and— from their chancy encounters—as Chicago detectives know especially well to do, Tim exited. But he knew full well and much too late that he should have kissed her that first time even though he had been sweaty and had stunk to high heaven.

And he recalled the fact that the smell of men's sweat can keep a woman's menstrual cycles regular. Maybe . . . just maybe his sweat would have been all right— he looked at his watch—forty-two minutes ago. How can a man's life and opportunities change in less than an hour?

He should have kissed her then. He should have pulled her against his sweaty, hot body and kissed her mindless. And if she'd objected to how he smelled, he could have taken her into the shower with him, clothes and all. It could have—it might have been okay.

Tim went dragging up the stairs, back to his apartment. Clean and slicked down, he sat at his computer and wrote one hell of a bloody chapter in which the hero rescues the heroine from a fate worse than death with the spook who was his nemesis, who had escaped his grasping hands, yet again. And the frustrated fictional hero showed the heroine what she'd almost experienced with the spook; but with the hero, she loved it.

With that, Tim stopped tapping away and sat glumly frustrated and irritated and looked out the gloomy window at the lousy day. It was a shared experience. The lousy day looked back, and neither the man nor the weather changed.

# Five

Meanwhile, down in her studio, Carol was patiently waiting for the odd couple to leave. Then they fooled her. They weren't there to fritter away idle time on a rotten, gloomy wet day, they bought two of her watercolors. And those were of Ready!

The baseball watercolors seemed so incongruous for such a couple, and yet, at the games, there were all sorts of people of all sizes and shapes. And like the couple with excellent taste, who'd just made the purchases of Carol's talented ability, there were those fans who had never been physically fit.

Carol saw the sensitive couple to the door, inviting them to come again. They were charming.

Then Carol turned back to her empty apartment and was sour. She admitted she was furious with Tim for not kissing her when she had made it perfectly clear, with one look, that she had wanted him to kiss her.

Men can be unbearably stupid at the most epic times—or was it epically stupid at unbearable times? No matter.

She went to her drawing table and spent the rest of the afternoon drawing horror scenes. Those creations were all in some dark and dank ghastly putrid swamp where a streaked blonde was being harassed and was fleeing from various monsters, all of whom had some haunting similarity to Timothy Bolt... who had bolted at a crisis time in her life.

Men are insensitive and obtuse. They have no feeling of communication with the female species. She had given Tim every opportunity to kiss her and wipe out those blah kisses given her by Ready. She had told Tim she had been disappointed in Ready's kisses. She had told Tim that when Ready had kissed her, nothing had happened. The sky had not fallen. What more did Tim need? She had even looked at him! What did he do? He said he needed a shower.

Men.

Her lips tight and a frown on her forehead, she ground her teeth as she added Tim's subtle betraying resemblance to the ugly monster that loomed in the swamp and was a part of the decay.

She set the papers aside to dry and turned on the television. The game was on hold. Two men were talking about baseballs and how they are thrown. They were demonstrating how the pitcher held the ball between his fingers and where the fingers were placed by what ball seams for which kind of throw.

Carol wished she'd known they were going to do that so she could have taped it for the kids at home. Then after some commercials and more discussion about the weather, the same two men began to discuss bats.

The bats are made of ash. The two men told of how, on occasion, bats had been altered by players. They told how the grain of the wood is important to the strength of the bat. And they said that a good piece of ash was hard to find.

There was a knock on the door. Really, it was barely a tap. Carol knew it was Tim. She took her own sweet time going to the door and opened it as she lifted her chin and said a frosty, "Yes?"

It was Megen, who was already leaving.

Carol said, "Good. Come on in. How'd you get inside?"

"Thelma was leaving. She let me in."

"I need company. You couldn't have chosen a better time."

"You're not . . . busy?"

"No. Come on in."

"Is . . . Ready. . . .here?"

"No. Was the game called?"

"Yes."

Hastily, Carol went to the watercolors she'd put aside. She wasn't sure they were dry enough, so she spread them up on top of her cabinets, out of sight.

"You've been working?" Megen was rather sad and aimless.

"Yeah. What's the matter?"

"Nothing." Megen turned aside, looking at the floor. Her word tone was a sigh.

"Don't tell me that. Something's been bothering you for a while. You weren't up to snuff out in L.A. I haven't been paying enough attention. You're not yourself. What's wrong?"

"Oh, it's—"

And the outside doorbell rang.

Carol went over and punched the button. "Yes?"

"Hi. It's Ready. Can I come in?"

She almost said, "No." She did hesitate, but she reluctantly punched the button and said, "Sure."

Megen became agitated.

To comfort her, Carol said, "We'll talk later. Something is really bothering you. Maybe I can help. We'll let Ready stay a little while."

Megen gasped, "No..."

"I can't turn him out on a day like this." Carol was logical. "It'll be okay."

"I should leave—"

"Of course not." Carol was at her own door by then, opening it. "Hi, Ready," she said courteously.

He came inside with a slight smile. Then he grinned wider as he saw Megen. "I thought you might be here."

Megen regarded Ready with ghost eyes. "Yes."

Ready continued, "I went by your place to bring you along, but you weren't home. I bet myself a dime you'd already come over here. And—" he grinned as if he'd won a dollar "—here you are!"

Again, Megen said a soft, melancholy, "Yes."

Carol was still by the door, still holding it open as she listened to that exchange. She began to close the door in a slow, thoughtful way, and Tim arrived.

He gave Carol a quick glance to see if she was still mad at him, and he got inside her apartment before she could object. He said to Ready, "Hi. I saw your car."

"Well, hi, yourself! How's the book coming?"

As Tim replied to that, Felix came out from the bedroom and sat down. He was followed by Phoebe, and Caruso trailed in last. They sat in a group as if they were discussing the adult humans. They tilted and turned their heads as if they were speaking inaudibly, which

Carol suspicioned they did quite well. Their discussion was amusing to them but not particularly kind.

Ready squatted down and patted Felix along his side as one does a dog. Felix moved out of reach. Ready stayed squatted and asked, "What did you girls have planned for this afternoon? How about a movie?"

"Where?" Tim asked.

Ready's smile was wide, "Here!" And he produced a copy of the film *Bull Durham* from his pocket. Somehow, none of the others was surprised by Ready's choice.

There weren't too many films one could see more than three times, but it just so happened that *Bull Durham* was still good after the tenth time.

Tim was very busy being host. He knew where everything was, and he helped and anticipated and showed Ready that he was the one who belonged at Carol's side. All the while, Tim surreptitiously watched Carol's reactions and movements and comments like the detective he was.

But who could figure women?

Tim could see no hostility to himself in Carol's attitude. Some aloofness was there, but she didn't actually reject him. In fact, she was deliberately but rather exaggeratedly a little coolly polite to him. He took that as a good sign. At least she wasn't indifferent.

And Ready was careful with Megen, talking to her as one does to a leashed and reluctant wild wolf. It was as if he felt confident that, with patience, he could communicate with her.

Carol began to be amused. She didn't want Ready. Megen didn't know that and was being careful. Carol was then surprised—she didn't want Ready? Had she ever? With some nostalgia that was obviously misplaced, Carol looked at the baseball player.

He was certainly beautiful to draw. He was a marvelous man, an amazing athlete. There. That was the attraction. She'd never wanted him.

Tim saw Carol's sentimental contemplation of his rival. Her study was poignant. Ready was coaxing Megen to sip some of his wine. Megen's eyes were downcast and she was struggling to appear indifferent. Tim already knew that Megen was fully zonked on Ready.

Even if Tim hadn't been so wrapped up in his own emotions over Carol, he would have realized that, out in L.A., when Megen had kissed Ready goodbye.

Tim searched his soul. He hadn't made any headway with Carol. She wanted Ready. The only thing Tim could do was help his love find her own love, Ready. Tim's soul shivered with the course he'd chosen.

But he loved Carol enough to help her to her happiness. Then he looked at Ready and knew Ready would never appreciate Carol as he should. He would seriously warn Ready to treat her right.

The movie was good as always, and Carol had snacks to serve. They managed a conglomeration of strange foods for supper. They were quite comfortable. Well, Ready was comfortable. Of the other three, Tim was edgy, Carol was exasperated and Megen was grieving.

Ready was saying, "How about it? If the game is called for tomorrow, how about coming with me to take Felix back to the farm? We can all go. You girls can sit in the back." He smiled as if they'd been offered a real deal.

Carol opened her mouth to decline a two-hundred-mile round trip in that backseat, and Megen said, "If Carol wants to, I will."

And Carol was caught in a bind. She would have to go so that Megen could see where Ready lived and see his family and have the opportunity to judge him from that angle. She would have to go. Hell.

Tim asked, "Why don't just you two go? You don't need Megen and me along."

He saw the flicker of dismay in Megen's eyes, so he didn't see the same dismayed response in Carol's.

With no indication that he'd been thwarted already, Ready said cheerfully, "We'll all go."

So through stiff lips, knowing all her muscles would be stiffer tomorrow, Carol agreed, "We'll all go." And she gave Tim a shriveling look.

He squinted his eyes, trying to figure out why. She'd looked at him like he'd done something stupid.

Then Tim did something marvelous. He said, "We'll rotate so that no one has to sit more than a half hour anywhere. Can you girls drive?"

Both said they could.

The next day, the game was called. They were all ready. They started out with Tim driving. That was predictable. But then in the rotation, Megen drove and she was a hell-on-wheels driver! They all protested.

Tim said, "I'm walking."

Carol said, "My God, Megen, you didn't drive that way at school!"

Megen said, "This car gets away from me."

And Ready asked, "What's wrong with the way she drives?"

So Megen didn't drive after that. They only allowed her to rotate to the passenger seat in front. And the men did ride in the back. They both took up too much room and they complained a lot.

Felix didn't seem to mind the return trip. He was in Phoebe's carrier, and he blinked his eyes and snoozed and paid no attention to the humans occupying another kind of carrier. Their vehicle was similar to his own confinement.

But Tim arranged Carol and curled her sideways against his own curled body, and knowing full well that he was going to give her up to Ready, Tim asked her, "Which way is Temple?"

"Over in Ohio, near Cleveland."

"I've never been over that way."

"It's pretty."

"When are you going home again?"

"Not until Thanksgiving."

"Oh." He was silent a while. Then he said, "It must be nice to have a family like that."

"You don't?"

"No. My mom took off when I was little. My dad died a couple of years ago. He never really recovered from the wounds he got in Korea."

"Was he in the Army?"

"No. The Navy." And Tim bit his lip because he'd almost said his dad had served with Salty on the same ship.

No one kept track of the time, Megen and Ready talked in the front seat and laughed some. And in the cramped back, Tim shifted Carol and asked her questions and listened and watched her, and he could brush his hands along her body, and he had the excuse to watch her mouth.

They finally arrived at the entrance to the Farthington farm. As they drove down the farm lane, Carol complained that she'd never had her turn at driving and she'd been in the cramped back more than she should have been.

That led to a good argument that stretched out. They got out of the car then, stretching themselves, and Carol rubbed her back. Tim watched her as if he were on the verge of helping her, but he did not.

Felix was released from his carrier and he, too, stretched and licked before he looked around and started off for the barn.

Ready's family was avidly curious about their guests, and they tried tactfully to sort out which was the woman who interested Ready, but they couldn't be sure. Felix had visited Carol, but Ready was explaining people and buildings to Megen.

The rest of the family had been notified of the visit, and the Farthingtons were all there. They were cheerful and kindly. Really, they were all very pleasant. The guests ate supper with the Farthingtons and overate. The Farthingtons laughed a lot over Felix's adventures in the big city. And they all watched to see which woman carried Ready's regard.

They knew about Tim's interest in Carol. He was so obvious. But if Carol was Ready's love, that would make the family nervous about Ready's chances. They didn't want him hurt.

So one uncle was designated to inquire of Tim just whom did Ready favor?

And Tim replied soberly, "Carol."

"Well, now," the uncle said. "You ought to back off."

"I have." Tim was serious.

"If this is 'backed off,' we'd hate to see what your 'interest' would be."

"She loves Ready."

The uncle frowned at Tim and said, "You must be stupid."

But Tim thought it was because he wasn't trying for the gem who was Carol, so he just nodded in agreement.

When it came time for the foursome to return to Chicago, Felix was in the car.

That caused a flurry of exclamations. "Now, have you ever in this world seen that cat in a car... voluntarily?"

And another Farthington questioned, "Why do you suppose he's in the car?"

So Carol said, "Phoebe."

The Farthingtons pished and toshed. "He has a HAREM here. He doesn't need a city cat!"

Carol shrugged and said something that was applicable to them all. "There's no accounting for taste."

That made Tim look at Ready, who was smiling beatifically at Megen. Tim closed his eyes over the pain Carol must feel if she should see that look. Tim suspected Carol was now aware that Ready's interest had been attracted to Megen. Carol was suffering. That was the reason Carol hadn't wanted to come on this visit. She would have to watch as Ready watched Megen. Her heart must be as shredded as the box that first brought Felix to Chicago.

Tim became pensive. See what love did to a male? Felix hadn't wanted to leave the farm, now here he was, in the car, waiting to go back to Phoebe.

And here was Timothy Bolt, slowly shriveling away because his woman loved another man and was suffering that man's rejection of her.

Poor Carol.

Carol got into the driver's seat. One of the uncles said something cheerily to Tim, and while those words were exchanged, Ready got into the cramped back of the Corvette with Megen—and the uncle chuckled low in his throat. Tim then realized that he was the uncle who had told him he must be stupid. In what way? Tim said the last goodbye and eased into the front passenger seat.

Tim looked over at Carol, who was laughing at something said to her by those standing around the car. She looked so good to Tim's eyes. To his senses. To his sex. He shivered a little.

She turned, still smiling, and asked Tim, "You ready for this?"

"Yes." He didn't care what.

"You must realize that I intend driving all the way back?"

He was forced by his good sense to inquire, "You do have a driver's license?"

"Yep."

Then he smiled just a little and said softly, "Let 'er rip."

With everyone yelling and calling goodbyes, with Felix licking and licking and licking, trying to get the smell of stranger cats off him before he saw Phoebe, Carol eased that fabulous car away from the crowd.

The car drove like a graceful bird about to take flight, skimming along the weed-crowded, unpaved access road. They came to the highway, and she stopped. There was no traffic. She eased onto the hard road, and the flight to Chicago was low and smooth and perfect.

No one else asked to drive. The two in back were talking in murmurs, laughing softly. Felix continued to lick, getting spruced up for Phoebe. Tim stretched his arm along the tops of the seats under the headrests, and he watched Carol, knowing that, if he wanted, he could move his hand a little and touch her.

They had one pit stop for gas, but they continued as they were, the two in the back, with Carol and Tim in the front.

The city traffic slowed them a bit, and it was just under two hours when they arrived back at Carol's place...and Tim's.

Ready exclaimed, "We're here already?"

Tim's glance sought Carol. Did she really hear that?

Megen said, "How fast did you drive?"

And Carol said, "Thirty miles per hour. It's 2:00 a.m."

"Really?" Megen's was a nothing response. The two in the back seat accepted that it was early morning. They didn't even look at their watches. They looked at each other and laughed.

Tim groaned for Carol. Could she be so blind that she couldn't see their attraction for each other?

Felix had his paws on the car's windowsill, looking at the house.

Ready asked, "Got everything? I'll say good-night here. I'll take Megen home."

Megen was forced to say, "My car's here."

Without hesitating, Ready amended, "I'll follow you home. It's late."

Tim said, "It's only ten o'clock."

"We'll see you at the game tomorrow?" Ready stood by his car. Felix was at the house door, and the two occupants of the house were on the sidewalk.

"I'm going to the game." Megen said that softly as she went toward her own car.

"I'll go with you," Carol said easily.

And Tim said with some anguish, "I'll be there." How would it be for Carol when it finally dawned on her that Ready was in love with Megen? Tim HAD to go along so that he could help her through that anguish, that hurt. Should he tell her now and save her, perhaps, from the additional pain of embarrassment?

The Corvette slowly pulled away, following Megen's car closely... very like Felix followed Phoebe.

Felix turned and looked at them impatiently. He said a meow that had about fifteen *r*'s in it. Then he yowled, and in Carol's window to one side of the porch, Phoebe appeared. She said a little anxious mew. And she was very alert and straining to see, moving her head quickly.

"Let's go in." Tim took Carol's arm.

"It's becoming a lovely night. Look at the clouds."

"It's going to rain again." He got out his key to the front door and inserted it.

"I'm full of kinks. I would love to walk around the block a couple of times."

"I'll go with you. Let me put Felix inside."

"If my door isn't to be shredded, you'll have to put him in with Phoebe." Then she leaned down and said to an attentive Felix, "I probably won't tell Phoebe how long you were in the barn."

The raunchy cat looked back at the door, waiting for the first crack so that he could push inside.

They went inside, and Carol opened her own door. She pushed it aside, and Felix went in to stand still. From the windowsill Phoebe watched him intently. She came down from the sill with a graceful drop before she moved toward Felix in a marvelous, feminine weave, to within several feet of him, and he waited. She sat down, and they watched each other.

"If we don't want to be embarrassed, we probably should go for that walk," Tim suggested.

"You know about the birds and the bees?"

"Yeah." And even as he replied, he thought that was a rather sassy comment coming from a discarded woman. And she was going out to walk with him. Maybe she wasn't as blind to what was going on between Ready and Megen as he'd thought. Maybe she knew it vividly and was going to seduce him in some sort of revenge for being shunned. He could handle that.

They closed her door and went back outside.

They were accosted just around the second corner. The guy wasn't alone, but Tim was so wound up that he was formidable. He slammed one against the building spread-eagled, and made the other lie facedown on the sidewalk. He threatened them horribly. They held there, afraid to move until the police came.

The two automatically began to wail, "Police brutality!" and "We wasn't doing nothing!" and "Thank God you came and saved us."

The police said, "Well, Jamie, you been out too long? Couldn't stay away? Need to be back inside?"

And the police said, "Ahhh, Bolt, how're you doing? We miss you, hanging around down at the station doing nothing all day. You cornered these guys all by yourself? Showing off for the lady? I know. She helped."

But Tim complained, "I never have any help at all. Where's the guys that's supposed to watch around here?"

The gathering neighbors chimed in, giving the cops a hard time. It was all cheerful and weird.

Carol got to go down to the station and give her statement. She went in Tim's car with him. At the station, many of the people who worked there spoke to Tim in that same rough, bantering way.

It all took a while, and it was some time before they were on their way back to the house. Carol said to Tim, "They like you."

"Yeah." He wondered if that surprised her.

"It's very late."

Sadly, he said, "Yeah."

"You were extraordinarily stupid to have attacked two hostile men."

"No."

"I thought I was going to have to scream and get some help for you. I might even have had to take a hand in the fracas."

He questioned in a soft voice, "Take a hand?"

"To help you. Two against one isn't fair."

"Don't you EVER interfere if I am attacked or am attacking. You could louse me up."

Superiorly, she mentioned in carefully enunciated words, "I've taken defense judo."

"Good for you."

"Do you detect a bit of hostility still lingering in your attitude?"

He shifted in his seat and glanced at her. "You be careful."

"Why?"

"I might have to show you what happens to sassy women."

"I can't believe this. You've always been a gentleman. A reasonable facsimile of one, that is, and—"

"Reasonable . . . facsimile?"

Since he questioned her, she felt she needed to explain. She comforted him. "You can pass as one."

In a very dangerous tone, he said, "Whoop-de-doo."

She studied him a little and said in that same snippy way, "I don't believe you're actually civilized."

"Enough."

"For what?"

"What I need."

She watched him more cautiously. And she didn't ask what he needed. They drove in silence.

He didn't let her out in front of the house. He drove around and through the alley to their car slots. Her car was still there and intact. The lighting was good. He pulled into his slot and he said, "Wait."

He got out of the car, locked the door and looked around. Then he came to her side and unlocked her door. He took her arm and helped her out.

She didn't need any help and slid out lithely. She was coordinated and her muscles were toned nicely. She was pleased with the way she moved, but she was now conscious of how she moved.

He pulled her to him and kissed her.

He really kissed her. He kissed her as he should have that rainy morning. He had never in this world intended taking advantage of her. He was furious with himself, but she'd just been so snippy, and he'd been so frantic over anyone threatening her safety that he'd not been cautious.

He held her precious body to his sensitive one and shuddered a little over the fact that she was all right. His emotions were borderline. He wanted to take her to his place, to his bed, so that he could protect her and keep her.

She might not want to go with him.

# Six

Carol pressed her hands to Tim's chest, indicating she wanted to be released. His iron will commanded his hands to do that, and only by demanding they obey did his hands release her.

Under the alley light, Carol looked oddly green. It was the light, but his writer's imagination made her a space alien. She was so different from any other woman he'd ever known. Within very loose bounds, women were predictable, as far as a guy could fathom the female sex. But with study, a man almost thirty could pretty well predict a woman. Not Carol, though. Carol was different. What if she really was an alien?

He'd go back, wherever it was, with her.

He looked around. Although he appeared as he always had, checking out the vicinity, he was actually thinking what a good world this was and that he would miss it.

He followed her to the back entrance and took his key out first. "You ought to have your key ready before you get to the door."

"Yes, sir."

She had a good attitude. She might be trainable. He looked down at her, glanced around and looked at her again. He wondered if he could possibly kiss her again or if he would have to wait until tomorrow.

As they entered the back door of the house, he asked, "Want to jog with me in the morning?" Then he thought of all the ways they could exercise together, and he lost track of the conversation.

She asked, "Together?"

Having forgotten what he'd asked, he rather elaborately closed the door after them and tested it to be sure it was secure. For all he knew, she might be suggesting they sleep together.

When he didn't reply, she elaborated, "Men jog at a different pace. I believe I should go alone." She led the way down the hall.

He followed her. "No."

She looked back over her shoulder and observed, "You've reverted." Then she faced forward again, and he got to watch down her back as she walked along in front of him. She had a great body.

She was alien, no question. "Reverted?" he asked. "To what?"

"Since I've known you these months, you've carried the facade of a writer—harmless, interested, slightly distracted. But now you're all cop—brief communication, suspicious, excessively male—"

If she wanted *male*, he could handle that.

"Frightening." She'd added that. They had reached her door. She turned and stood there, looking at him, blocking his entrance.

"I scare you?" He was appalled.

"Something makes my stomach shiver."

Well, now— He put his hand just under her breasts. His voice reedy, he asked, "There?"

"No."

The lights in his green eyes changed. He licked his lips. Tonight was the night. He moved his hand around as if searching for the spot, but his thumb slid along the underside of her breasts. Then he forced it down about two inches and asked in a definitely husky voice, "There?"

She took his hand and gave it back to him as she said, "No." Then she put her readily available key into her door lock and opened it. "Good night." She gave him a flick of a glance.

But he blocked the door's closing and said, "You're on the ground floor. Let me check the windows."

In a droll manner, she gave him a cynical look and commented, "I've been here quite a while. In and out on various occasions. No one has had to check the windows for me before now."

He looked at her, thinking of all the times he'd done exactly that. "Let me."

"What?" Her eyes rounded.

And not asking what she meant, his busybody tongue just went on and said, "Check the windows."

She gave him a disbelieving look and guessed: "You want to see if Felix has died of exhaustion, right?"

Now, why would she want to drag sex into the conversation? His eyelashes closed down a bit and his mouth smiled slightly. His sensitive tongue licked his upper lip very slowly from one side to the other as his mind raced around, trying to find something clever to say. His whole mental file of quick-witted repartee was empty.

He was a writer. Think! He said lamely, "I hate digging cat graves after midnight. The sound of a shovel attracts unwanted attention. You generally have to show the cat's body, and since they have nine lives, they've almost always gotten up and left. We'll have to decide if it's a true death and final, or if he's just 'plumb wore out.'"

She laughed the softest, most delighted sound. It curled his toes and straightened everything else.

She said, "Good night. Thank you for not insisting on your turn at driving the Corvette."

"You're welcome."

"Get your foot out of the door."

He looked down in some contrived surprise. "Oh. Sorry. Jogging at six...seven? Eight?" He was offering whatever she wanted.

"Not tomorrow. We've promised to watch baseball tomorrow. I'll have to work."

"Yeah."

Again she said, "Good night."

He looked at his watch. "It's only begun. It isn't even midnight yet."

She just smiled, amused by him, and she closed the door.

She listened. But his soft steps on the stairs were some time coming. Why had he stood outside her door? What had he been thinking? She hummed a little as she went about getting ready for bed.

Felix was dead to the world in the middle of her bed. Phoebe was beside him. She blinked at Carol and purred.

"You're a fallen female." Carol sighed with impatience. "He's just visiting. You have to realize that. A barn cat! You have no taste at all. It makes me wonder about you, Phoebe."

Phoebe licked a paw and slowly rubbed it behind her ear, very like a smug woman patting the hair at the back of her head.

Before she got into bed, Carol pulled Felix over to the side.

With the movement, Phoebe jerked up in indignation.

Carol said precisely, "It is my bed. Not his."

Phoebe spat at her!

"I don't understand you. Who's fed and cared for you all this time? Just because that barn cat comes along and romances you, you want him to have the middle of my bed!"

Phoebe lay like the statue of the Egyptian lion and looked sternly at Carol.

"You're spoiling that barn cat simply because you like sex. I am shocked."

Phoebe's stare was censuring. Then she turned her head slowly and ignored the stupid woman who was settling herself in the cats' bed. As usual, the woman was trying to hog the middle. Phoebe blinked. It wouldn't take long for the three cats to crowd her over. They did that every night.

In the murky dawn, Carol's phone rang. Fortunately she was on that edge of the bed and could pick it up without too much trouble. She said, "Yes?"

"Wanna jog?"

"You lecher!" she mumbled and hung up.

She didn't waken again until after ten. She was disgusted. She went into her studio with her nightgown still on and her hair a streaked tumble and viewed what she was to do that day. She called Megen. "I can't play today. I have to work."

"What a work ethic you've acquired."

Carol was patient. "That sounds like a woman living on great-granddaddy's money."

"It's convenient," Megen assured her friend. "Did you notice the sky is clearing? They'll play."

"Who will pl—Oh, baseball."

"Where's your mind?"

"Not here." Carol was sure. "Give my regards to the team. Cheer twice as loud to make up for my not being there. Kiss Ready for me."

"......yes."

"You faded away there. What did you say?"

Soulfully, Megen replied, "I'd forgotten."

"What was that?"

"I'll call you later."

"We never got to talk about you," Carol complained. "Are you all right?"

"I think I'll go to California and see Mother."

"Now, you have to know her solution to any problem."

Megen cautioned, "Don't be nasty."

"I'm honest. Let me advise you."

"I already know what you'd suggest, Carol. You'd tell me to get a job or do volunteer work."

"What a good idea!"

"I find you very irritating today, Carol. Perhaps we can speak on another day."

"Uh-oh."

"Goodbye, Carol, I know you mean well. Good luck with Ready." And she gently placed the phone in its cradle.

"Ready?" Carol frowned at the picture of her great-grandmother who stared back coldly. Carol put her hands into her hair and strained to think why Megen should wish her luck with Ready. After those two had spent most of that trip home from seeing Ready's folks in Porter County, rolling around in the back of the Corvette, why would Carol want him back?

Megen couldn't have meant that. She probably said "Good luck TO Ready" because the team would play today. It was only soggy out. No more rain was falling. Everything was steamy and damp and awful. But that was great for the farmers because such weather was good for growing corn.

Carol went into the hall, and there was Phoebe crouched down, her tail hooked aside, and she was looking at Felix.

Felix spared one cool glance at Carol to verify her as not counting for anything; then he took a step around Phoebe. She hissed gently at him and didn't move.

As Carol went by the cats, she leaned over and said in a firm voice, "You're going to get very pregnant if you continue this foolish behavior. When you have to waddle around and can't jump up on the bed by yourself, remember what I've said."

Laying her ears back, Phoebe steam-hissed at Carol, and Felix gave a low, warning growl.

That made Carol indignant. "Whose house is this?" She waved a hand. "You're a couple of freeloaders!"

But then she remembered how long it had been since she'd seen a mouse. How irritating, that she would think of the lack of mice at this crucial time of moral confrontation.

So she said to Felix, "I see no reason to have Phoebe submit to you just because you showed my cats how to catch mice."

Felix ignored her, but Phoebe blinked her eyes at the humorous statement that she belonged to Carol.

Bathed, dressed in jeans and a shirt, Carol was ready for the day just before noon.

She spent that day in drawing the barn cat. When he wandered off, she would go get him, and put him back on the forest green pillow. He would lick and he would yawn and he would relax like a tree lion and watch her with lazy yellow eyes. Mostly, he slept.

How like males to prowl until they're satisfied.

Ready called her about four and told her, "You've got to find Megen. She's going to California." Then he called in an aside, "Okay!" And he came back to Carol and said, "She thinks I'm in love with you."

"Now, how could she think that?"

"I guess when I kissed you out in California."

"Oh."

"Stop her."

"Can't you do that?"

He shouted in indignation, "I've got to play ball!"

Annoyed, Carol asked, "Where is she?"

"Going to the airport."

"Which one?"

"I don't know!"

Frustrated, Carol said, "Hell."

But Ready had hung up.

So Carol called Tim. "How do I find out which airport Megen's in?"

"Why?"

It was a logical word, but it irritated the liver out of Carol. "She is going to see her mother because she thinks Ready loves me."

"He doesn't?" Tim asked cautiously.

"Of course not."

"But—"

"He was only feeling guilty for his bat hitting my thigh. We are unsuited."

She *knew* that? "Yes."

"If you have no ideas on how to do this, I have to get off the phone and try someone else."

"You call Megen first."

"She could go on any plane at all!"

"If you can't get hold of her, don't worry, I got some friends."

"I'll try."

"Call her house first."

So Carol did and got hold of Megen there. "Come over here, Megen. You have Ready upset with your leaving. You're acting unstable. We have to sort you out."

"You think *I'm* un—"

"Don't argue like you always do, just come over here. I can't go out, running all over the airports, trying to find you just because Ready can't g—"

"Why can't he?"

*"He has to play ball!"* Carol said that through her teeth and at a rather impressive volume. To do that between clenched teeth took talent. She said in a low and warning voice, "You come here. I'm working. You butterflies are a nuisance."

"Butterflies?"

Carol snapped, "All play and no work."

"Those are grasshoppers."

"Don't be nit-picking, come over here so I can quarrel with you."

"You're doing a fairly good job of it on the phone."

"Don't go hostile." Carol snapped. "I have to call off Tim and his cohorts who are trying to track you down."

"The police?"

"Who else?"

"Good God Almighty. You're hysterical."

"Not me. Ready."

"He . . . was?"

"You idiot!"

"You have a very strange way of being a friend. You could use a better choice of words for starters."

"Megen . . . *Come over here!*"

"All right."

Carol shouted: "Now!"

"I said, all right!"

"Then DO IT!"

They hung up with no further words, and Carol called Tim. "Megen was at her place. You need to cancel the people—"

"I haven't called anyone."

"You . . . haven't?"

"No. People who warn other people they are leaving and want to be stopped from doing that wait around to be stopped."

After a silence, Carol mentioned, "I believe I'll go with the astronauts to the moon the next time . . . and stay there."

"You'd fit in anywhere."

She was distracted. "How do you mean that?"

"Is Megen coming over?"

"Yeah." She got that word out of the way so that she could ask again, "How did you mean that about me—"

"I'll come down and explain Ready to Megen."

"How will you do that?"

He replied, "Women aren't sensitive."

There was a pithy silence. "Tim—"

"And eventually, I'll explain women to you."

That irritated her the most.

So when Megen arrived, Carol wasn't in the most tactful of moods. She said, "Ready wants you to stay here and admire him."

That made Megen indignant.

Carol's apartment door opened, and Tim walked in. Carol ignored him, she was so concentrated on Megen. Carol said to Megen, "Sit down. I want to point something out to you. See these drawings?"

"Marvelous, as always. Carol, you have tal—"

Carol was lecturing Megen. "Ready is a barn cat. Look at him and compare him with Felix." She took some watercolors of Ready and put them next to those of Felix.

Megen held still for it. She did compare them. She picked up one of Ready with caring hands, and her face was gentle as she said, "Ready's ears are intact."

With endurance, Carol pointed out, "Look at Felix." She moved the watercolor of the cat alongside her watercolor of Ready that Megen held. Carol urged, "See?"

Megen examined the two diverse creatures. "They're both redheaded."

Carol held firm and was only positive. "Look at them. They're both barn cats. They are basic males."

Megen had the gall to say confidently, "I think I've caught him in time." And she gave Carol a tolerant look.

But Tim laughed. He was so amused. Megen turned and smiled at Tim with such knowledgeable kindness, and he laughed some more. Carol gave him an exasperated look and frowned, but that only made Tim really guffaw.

Carol wondered why women needed men around at all.

Choosing her words precisely, Megen said, "Neither of you is to say anything about this meeting between us. And you are not to mention that I came willingly. Do you understand? If Ready and I are to be serious and survive, he must be so sure about loving me that he will convince me that he is earnest."

So Tim asked, "Who's Ernest?"

Neither woman felt the need to reply or to explain.

The phone rang. Carol answered. It was the ticket booth at Wrigley Field. "Ready left three tickets here for you and two others. He said to call you. The tickets are for tonight's game."

"I hadn't realized it was a doubleheader."

That amazed the ticket man.

At the end of the conversation, Carol hung up the phone and told the two attentive eavesdroppers, "Today's game is a doubleheader."

Tim nodded as if everyone was aware of that.

Carol continued, "Ready left three tickets for tonight's game at the ticket office for us." She looked at Tim with the residue of distaste that his hilarity had left in her mouth. She said, "One ticket is for you." She made it sound as if they would be seated separately.

Megen stated neutrally, "When people are courting, they become prickly with each other's conduct."

Tim nodded.

Carol said, "Bosh."

Megen commented from the point of view garnered by age and experience, "If Tim had disagreed, you'd have agreed."

Carol looked at Megen as if she was refraining from calling attention to Megen's second, sprouting head.

Although Tim offered to treat them to hot dogs and beer at the game, Carol fixed them each a salad. She had to add more of everything when it became clear that Tim expected to share their meal. She served croutons with the salad and cups of hot boullion.

Tim got up and made himself a sandwich of peanut butter, nuked bacon, cheese and tomatoes with lettuce.

With such easy conduct from Tim, Carol was elaborately patient and markedly silent. She spoke of things to Megen that Tim knew nothing about. In turn, Megen explained Carol's references nicely to the attentive man.

Since the rain had made the air very humid, the evening coolness would be damp and penetrating. Tim mentioned that and suggested the women dress accordingly.

The only reason Carol obeyed was because Tim went up to his apartment to change and get a jacket. With him gone, she could appear to make her own decision.

Megen observed, "You can be a real bitch."

"Nonsense."

"I have observed conduct in you this day that gives every indication you are entrapped by Timothy Bolt."

"Don't be any more ridiculous than you already are."

"Do you suppose we'll ever discuss this time when we are old and reminiscing in rocking chairs."

And Carol replied, "By then we won't be speaking at all."

Megen laughed softly but with such humor that Carol was forced to smile. Carol admitted, "I don't know what's the matter with me."

"You are attracted to Tim, but you don't want him to know."

Carol scoffed. "That would be self-defeating."

"You're worse than I was."

"You're no longer difficult?"

"Not lately."

"Only as early as this afternoon?"

"I thought you wanted Ready, and you saw him first."

"But you drove down to meet his family."

"I was trying to discourage myself. He's so marvelous. I've wanted him since the first time I saw him. I showed you a pitcher so you wouldn't notice Ready. But you drew all those pictures of Ready. Then his damned bat hit you! Why couldn't it have hit me?"

Thoughtfully, Carol observed, "I don't believe I've ever heard of anyone who complained about not being hit by a bat before this very minute."

Megen suggested, "Tonight, see if you can act ordinary, or at least reasonably close to that?"

"I will try."

"How kind."

But Carol hurried out first and got into the backseat of Tim's car. As Megen slid into the front seat, she gave a look at Carol that ought to've chilled her to the bone.

Carol returned a bland look. Then she realized Tim could see her perfectly well in the rearview mirror, and she blushed.

Tim was very cordial to both women, but he treated Carol as if she was behaving. She gritted her teeth and wondered how any man could be so excruciatingly dense?

As they came to their excellent seats, Carol crowded by and went in first so that Megen would sit between her and Tim. But Megen stepped back, and Tim sat between them.

Carol accepted the hot dogs and the beer that Tim garnered for the three of them. She was so aware of Tim beside her that she ate the ballpark fare without noticing it. She gulped down the cold beer, and what with one thing or another, she got a chill.

She tried to minimize the shivers, but it was impossible. She shifted and moved and clenched her teeth to keep them from rattling.

Tim stood up, took off his jacket and said, "Here. You drank the beer too fast."

That wasn't offensive. She took the jacket and it was still hot from his heat. She shrugged into the jacket and wrapped his heat around her. It was marvelous. She smiled just a little and hugged his jacket to her.

And he had the stupid audacity to add, "You ought to know better than to drink cold beer that fast."

She sat there blankly, trying to figure a plausible way to get out of the park and back to her apartment, without crawling over Tim who would probably want to know where she was going.

She looked down the other way, and it was much too far with too many people to crawl over. Tim would notice if she went that way and would probably object and cause a scene.

In her ear, he said, "Sit still and behave, or I'll take you out to the car and give you something else to think about."

She didn't look at him or reply. She wondered what he had in mind.

It was a good ball game, most of which Carol didn't see or register at all. She sat there and sorted through her life to discover why she was sitting next to this despicable man at a baseball game on a cold, clammy night when she could be comfortably at home.

The time came to stand up for the seventh-inning stretch. They did that, sang The Song and settled down again. It was an endless game that lasted just over two hours.

Two hours?

She'd never seen a game accomplished in such a short time. What had happened? It was the top of the ninth, the score was three to two in favor of the Cubs. The enemy was batting. They had one man on and the go-ahead man was batting. There were two outs.

The man at bat was a whiz-bang hitter. Everyone was in place. He hit the next pitch, which bounced toward Ready, and Ready stretched and caught it, but he fell to his left knee. However, he didn't scramble. He continued with the fall to roll, rise and throw in one spectacular movement. He threw it perfectly. The man was out. The game was over. The Cubs won. Bedlam ensued.

There may have been a dribble of spectators who did leave at that time, but not anyone else. They all stood yelling and waving their arms and carrying on like mad people, hugging and jumping up and down. And Carol turned to Tim, laughing up at him, and she hugged him.

He didn't let go.

She stood within his warm embrace, still wearing his jacket, and she allowed him to hold her.

She said in shock, "I'm still wearing your jacket."

He replied, "That's okay. I'm hot enough."

She turned her head toward the field where the players were all pounding on each other and laughing. But she had turned her head not to watch the players but so she wouldn't ask Tim why he was hot.

She said quite low so that there was the possibility he wouldn't hear. "I'm sorry."

"About what?"

He'd heard. She elaborated a tiny bit. "I've been difficult."

"You're worth it."

What was she worth?

She didn't reply, and he didn't explain.

They weren't really any closer or clearer than they had been.

The trio had been directed as to where they would meet Ready, and they finally went there. He came out exuberant and just stood and laughed.

It was so wonderful for him to be amused by his spectacular catch instead of being smug. His parents were there, and some of his other kin. He took Megen's hand and introduced the three again to sort out who was who and with whom.

And Carol was with Timothy Bolt.

She looked up at his strong face and wondered at the remarkable chance that had put him into the same old house at that time.

It had been a miracle.

# Seven

The next morning at an unreasonable hour, Carol's phone rang. Carol lifted it and asked, "Yes?"

"Wanna jog?"

"Not that."

The phone clicked in Tim's ear, and her reply confused him. If not that . . . what? His mind spun away in its usual direction.

In something of a daze, he went out and ran someplace or the other, and only instinct got him home again. It was a drippy, nasty day and eighty degrees already. August in Illinois is always an experience. He and Carol were just lucky to be so close to The Lake.

Tim went back to the old house and looked at it with a critical eye. Even shabby, it was elegant. He looked around at the other houses. They'd been abused too long. In a few years, the whole neighborhood would come down, then some matchbox rabbit warrens would be erected and filled like an ant farm.

He went inside and saw that her door was open. Dripping sweat, he was again dank and smelly. He cautiously approached her door, just to peek inside.

He couldn't have made a sound, but she turned from her drawing table and looked at him. She didn't speak. She simply looked at him.

He *knew* now was the time, but he hesitated and was again reluctant.

His reluctance last time had caused the rift in their progression to passion. If he drew back now in order to shower, she might be ticked again.

He still hesitated.

She licked her lower lip, just a tiny, slow flick and then slid her wet lower lip up over her upper lip and just looked at him, so seriously.

He went slowly to her, and she didn't cough or choke over the smell of him. He lifted her off that stool, up against his wet, smelly body, and he kissed her like a woman should be kissed.

She gasped, and he was stunned. She moved a little, and he almost let her go, but her hands went up onto his wet shoulders, and her mouth was available. He kissed her again.

The whole universe was rearranged. Stars traded places and there were whirlings of light. It was just a good thing that Earth had that palm-tree brand there at the northern border of the U.S. of A. This world could still be sorted out, but the two human causes of all that chaos were still kissing.

He finally lifted his steaming face from hers with a mouth-squeak that shivered his entire libido. He looked into her eyes. He was hotter than a two-dollar pistol.

She murmured, "That was nice."

Nice? NICE! So he simply squeezed her sweet, soft body closer and kissed her again, not being so considerate. If those first kisses had been "nice" then he might not get another opportunity to try the other kinds. So he kissed that limp woman, and his hands moved and he blew off the top of his own head.

With his brains completely gone, Tim eased his mouth from Carol's and held her, looking down at her somnolent face. She was inert.

She was also boneless and putty in his hard hands. He molded parts of her. She simply allowed it. She'd gone to sleep? Fainted? He asked carefully, "Carol?"

She replied, "Ummmmm."

"What's that mean?"

"You...'re...pretty...good."

And his voice was indignant! "I'm terrific!"

"Yes," she agreed slowly. "You must have practiced on any woman who would hold still long enough for you to try."

"I did not. You're my first!"

She chuckled quite naughtily.

He protested: "I practiced on my hand—laying my thumb close along the side of the palm and then giving it wet kisses and push—"

She laughed, a delicious little sound in her throat. To Carol, her sound was very like some of the mews Phoebe said to Felix. Surely not.

With some determined effort, Carol stood on her own two feet. That was a feat. She wiggled her body marvelously against his to indicate that she wanted to be freed, and she made him groan and hesitate before loosening his arms.

She took a small half step back from him and gave him an owl-eyed look. Then she glanced out the window and said, "It's a lovely day."

He dumbly looked out on the corn-growing mess and blinked. Then he smiled down on his besotted love and he said, "Yes." That's when he was sure she was partial to him.

But she wouldn't allow him another kiss. She said prissily, "I have work to do."

She was dismissing him. But she hadn't scolded him or slapped him. She'd kissed him back. She hadn't said that he shouldn't kiss her or couldn't. She'd lain against his sweaty, smelly body and cooperated.

He'd shower and maybe he could get another kiss. More.

The idea of kissing her, of holding her against him again was riveting. His whole body shivered to be close to her. His sex wanted more than that. His mouth hungered for the taste of her. And he was unable to say anything except, "I'll be back."

She watched him with heavy eyelids and a slight little smile.

He could hardly climb the stairs to his apartment. As he washed his alert body, he gave intense thanks that in his rough life, he'd been cautious and careful.

Clean and slick, he went down the stairs, trembling a little, anticipating a lot, and nervous as a fifteen-year-old. Her door was still open.

He went inside and stood amazed. She was darting around, looking at pictures, putting her hands into her hair, excited...*but not by him!*

He asked, "What's the matter?" And his muscles hardened, ready to attack whatever or whoever had upset her.

"Oh, Tim! I've been invited to show at the Art Institute! It's a show of local artists. This is a coup!"

He was stunned. "That's great." His voice was flat, no enthusiasm. But he was smart enough to automatically add, "How can I help?"

"I get three pieces to show. What'll I choose? I'll have to look at everything I've done lately and figure it out. Oh, this is wonderful!"

He nodded.

She wasn't paying him any real attention. "One of Ready. Those are so popular. And one of the barn cat? Those two would be great side by side, the two are so marvelously similar."

Tim found he wasn't at all interested in her showing watercolors of another man.

Silently Tim watched as she forgot him. She pulled out papers and canvases and stacked them around or pinned them on the viewing cardboards leaning on the cupboards.

And Tim saw the edge of thick, unmistakable watercolor paper on the tops of one series of cabinets. "You must have put some watercolors up there to dry. I'll get them down for you."

Carol turned her head and stared. In slow motion she watched him get the stool and climb up to take down the horror pictures she'd done with Tim as the monster. He would see them. She realized what was happening. She gasped, frozen.

He looked at the first two and said, "I thought you didn't like horror. These are good! I'll have you illustrate my first—uh—"

She froze, simply horrified.

In a softer voice, he said, "These look a little like . . . me."

"No. Put them back."

He didn't hear her. He took down the others, looking at them sober-faced. He compared and studied.

She said, "Tim— I'd forgotten them up— You see—"

He looked at her blank-faced and asked, "When were you this mad at me?"

"Those aren't of you. I was just seeing if I could draw something else. Like I did the sea storm from my bruise. I saw the bruise and the colors—"

"And you were mad at me and made me into all the horrors. You are brilliant!"

She snapped at him. "You were nasty."

And he laughed.

"Tim—" Her tone was different. Serious. Saying his name was like gently touching his arm with her hand.

He heard it and looked at her. "You are so talented that you scare me a little. How can I help you to paint when I want all your time?"

"Tim—" She was melting.

"You have to know that I want you." He moved a step toward her.

Her eyes were filled with communications if only he could sort them all out. The need, the desire, the longing. But there was commitment in them, caution, recklessness.

Very softly he told her, "I'll take care of you." He moved another step toward her.

"I don't want to be the receiver, I want sharing."

"Yes." He smiled at her, put down the horrors and went to close her door and lock it. Then he turned and said, "I want to make love to you."

That rattled her a little. She began to babble a bit. He was so bold. If she went to him, he would know that's what she wanted, and it just seemed such a bald-faced wanting. He could be more subtle and— "You could be more subtle."

"Probably. But I'm a simple man. I've been in such a state over you. I didn't know how to approach you. I felt like a ragtag nothing by a princess, and I want to be a hero to you." He was closer.

"You are."

"It was Ready who solved the mice." He moved nearer.

"It was you who tackled two men all by yourself."

"That wasn't skill, that was pent-up frustration."

"Maybe I shouldn't make love with you. I might weaken you."

He laughed and then rubbed his hand over his face as he protested, "I would be involved and possessive and protec—"

"Possessive?"

"That's balanced by protective and whatever else it was I said, isn't it?"

"I'm not sure."

"Aren't you possessive? You've been a witch to me lately. Then you turned that sweet body against me at the ballpark last night and about sent me through the roof."

"That's lust."

"That's want. I want you. Not just now but for all time. Are you an alien?"

"No. My families have been around the Midwest for generations. Did you think I'd just sneaked across the border?"

"I think you're from outer space."

"Weird?" She frowned.

"Remarkable." He took her gently, cautiously into his arms. "Kiss me. Kiss me and tell me you love me."

But he didn't give her the time. He kissed her, and what he lacked in skill, he made up with earnestness. And he was earnest. He lifted her up and carried her back to her room.

All the cats were on the bed and they looked up with interest. He said, "Scat!"

They moved a little, but they didn't get off the bed.

So Tim swung her feet in their direction and said again, "Scat!"

The cats got out of the way, still not convinced until he placed her on the bed, swept them off the bed and shooed them out the door. He closed the door and turned back to her.

She said, "Uhhh."

And he smiled. "I've dreamed of having you just that way since you moved in."

"That was months ago."

"Only months? I've aged years, waiting for you to realize I'm the only man for you."

"You stood around taking notes at parties. You never paid any attention to me."

"I was watching over you. Remember Frank?" He pulled his shirttail out of his shorts.

"Frank?" She frowned.

Unbuttoning his shirt, he commented, "See? I knew his look. I sent him packing before he got entrenched. I've gotten rid of them all, but you scared the hell out of me with Ready. I thought I'd lost you."

"Ready? I only liked drawing him. Do you know his eyebrows are as varied in colors as his hair?"

Tim didn't want to talk about Ready at all. He asked, "What about mine?" He discarded the shirt and undid his shorts' band.

She peeked at that, but she replied, "There's a rift along your right eyebrow. The hairs grow differently. It gives you a dangerous look. Your eyes are beautiful."

"They're green like yours." He dropped his shorts and put his thumbs under his skivvies' band.

She blushed rather vividly, but she said, "Yours are darker green. They're jewels. Do you see in the dark?"

"Only you." He came to the bed and crawled to her rather tense body. "Have I ever told you how beautiful you are?" He lay beside her, propped on one elbow. His free big hand moved so that his fingers could touch her hair. He put a gentle finger on her cheek. "I very badly need to kiss you."

She swallowed.

He leaned over her and kissed her as he slowly moved, pushing with his mouth until she lay flat. The kiss then was spectacular. Was it really?

When he lifted his mouth, she said, "Again."

He complied. His free hand moved, loosening her clothing as his mouth very slowly changed angles and his tongue touched her lips. His hand slid under the loosened clothing and covered her naked breast, fondling, kneading gently. His breathing changed and his body became sternly controlled, except for a minute restlessness.

Her hands were in his hair, then on his shoulders and down his back. He moved against her, allowing her to feel the size of him. She gasped.

But he deepened his kissing and coaxed her to higher passion. She ventured cautiously.

He got her clothes off her so sneakily that she murmured, "How'd you learn to do that?"

And he replied, "Red Cross."

While she was puzzling that out—disaster training? drowning victims?—he managed to get rid of the rest of her coverings. But then he leaned back and looked at her lying there, naked as a jaybird.

He smiled and said, "You're more beautiful than I ever imagined."

And being Carol, she poofed that. "I'm just like any other woman."

He was smart enough to say, "I've not seen very many."

"Oh? Who?"

"Magazines?"

"Do you really expect me to believe that?"

"How many men have you been with?"

"None."

"Then why are you blushing so? Are you embarrassed to tell me?"

"No, silly, I'm not very big-chested and my hip bones protrude when I'm lying flat this way. I wish I could be soft and lovely."

"Ah, Carol, if you could only see yourself as the magic that I see you. You are the most beautiful woman in all the world."

She wasn't swayed and continued blushing. She was glad he had a condom. "You are smart."

But she stiffened and held her breath and was apprehensive over their coupling. He fooled her. With mighty self-discipline, he delayed.

He truly made love to her and sought carefully to coax her to passion. That wasn't too successful, but he'd caught her curiosity so that she helped his entry with earnest cooperation but not too much emotional involvement.

And he found out that, indeed, she had never been with another man.

They lay still as she adjusted to the reality of his weight and intrusive presence. He was breathing like an agitated bull, trembling and shivering, and he was filmed with hot sweat.

She lay, considering her position, and she said clinically, "That isn't too shocking."

There was a brief silence; then Tim began to laugh. He chuffed and leaned up on his elbows. He put his forehead against hers and his body shook with his laughter.

"What's so funny?" she inquired with interest.

"I wonder what an earnest man, who is totally involved in making love should do when the woman says something like that?"

"What?"

"You said this wasn't too shocking."

"Well, now, have you ever looked at yourself?"

"Did you look at me?"

"Every chance. You are fascinating. You're as big as a baseball bat!"

"Is that why women like baseball?"

"Think of being a woman and seeing a naked man in heat for the first time as—"

"I've been in heat before."

"I haven't seen it. And if you were the woman, even though you KNOW it's supposed to work and you see people in films moving and groaning and apparently liking it. And even though everyone SAYS it will, you can't be really sure that it will fit. And you must admit that it's a very intimate thing to do."

He agreed tenderly. "It's making love."

"Not all the time. Sometimes it's just having sex."

"I wouldn't know about that."

"You've always 'made love'?"

"With you."

"Now, Tim, you can't be a beginner. We know I was, but you're too sly and skilled."

"Sly?"

"How come you could lure me in here to bed just after the Art Institute has offered me a place in their show? How could you distract me like this if you weren't sly about it?"

"You're a closet sensualist?"

"Of course not. I'm ... well, I've always been an earnest artist ... before this day."

He smiled down at her and moved a little. "You like this?"

"It is interesting."

He carefully separated from her, and then he began to show her what her body could do to them both. He nuzzled and licked and suckled and encouraged her outrageous examination of him. He sucked in air and shuddered and breathed erratically and groaned. And she laughed a wicked, wicked laugh she'd never known she possessed.

He asked her huskily, "How do you know to laugh that way and set me on end?"

"You just taught me."

"I've never laughed that way in all my life. My vocal cords won't make that kind of sly sound."

She sassed, "You didn't *show* me, you taught me that when you instructed me in teasing."

"I believe you've been a tease all your life. It's genetic to your gender. I bet you've been doing that since you were—say—eight. I'll bet little boys pulled your pigtails, and you were indignant and sashayed around and put up your nose and peeked at them and—flirted.''

''Never. I read books.''

''On...'' he encouraged her response as he fiddled with her.

''On drawing, of course.''

''Ahhh. Of course.''

She said, ''Ummmm.'' And she said, ''Do that again.''

''This?''

''Oh, yes.'' Instinctively, she gave a counter move.

And he groaned.

''Did I hurt you?''

''Wonderfully.''

She scoffed and wiggled.

He gasped and groaned, ''Be careful!''

''Why?''

''I'm really triggered. I don't want to come until you can.''

''I'm not sure I can. This has been so strange that I've been distracted.''

''Well, I'll see if I can catch your attention without becoming too involved.''

She laughed.

''Now, what's funny about that? You have to know how risky it is for me to try to warm up a cold woman when I'm about to go off?''

''You said you didn't want to become involved.''

He laboriously managed to heist his shoulders up and brace himself on his elbows so that he could look into her face. ''You're not helping me one bit.''

''What should I do?''

"Groan and gasp and pretend you're going out of your mind with lust."

"What sort of groans?"

"Uhhhhh. Wellll. Like you're having to walk with a sprained knee."

Her groan was disbelief.

He complimented her, "That's it! Now do that for a while as I move around."

She groaned, but she spoiled the whole thing by then giggling.

So he kissed her to shut her up, and one thing led to another and they became riveted by the growing sensations. She began to gasp, and her hands tried to pull him closer.

Their brains were swamped with the magic of desire, and their bodies relished the building of the magical thrills. Then he tried to slow down and experience the ecstasy of the coupling, but she was lost to it. He had no choice but to ride it out on the wild winds of passion to paradise.

They wobbled as they landed back on the bed. Their breaths were erratic, their muscles flaccid and helpless, and their eyesight faulty. They lay spent.

After some time, she asked, "Why are you still lying on top of me?"

"I've had to keep you covered until you cooled so you wouldn't set off the smoke alarm."

She laughed. She giggled. She said, "You silly—" And she said, "Get off me, you lug."

Reluctantly, he rolled off her to one side and held her hand. "I've been thinking. No remarks on that, just listen. I've been thinking I could cut a circle in the ceiling here, up to my place, and I'd put in a fireman's pole. I could slide down any time you were handy."

"No."

He was indignant. "Now that you've had my body, you're tossing me aside?"

"Not necessarily, but I can't have my dad or mother walk in here and see a fireman's pole from your apartment. They may think it was a strange arrangement."

"We could explain how old the house is and how tinder dry, and that I need an alternate escape route."

"My dad was a boxer in the Navy, and he's mean."

"Yeah." Tim chuckled.

"Now, how did you know that?"

"Hmmm? Oh, all dads are mean to nice young men who love their wicked daughters."

"You . . . love me?" Her voice was shy.

"Haven't I spent this whole time demonstrating that?"

"I thought you were just curious about me."

"That, too. It's a good thing that pole isn't in place right now, I'd hate to have to shinny up it."

She put her hand on him. As he sucked in air in a shivering gasp, she said, "This pole's in place."

"Careful. You'll start something very serious."

"What?"

There are just things a man has to do when called upon to demonstrate facts. So it was an hour or so later when they lay again, depleted and smiling.

In an unoriginal way, he said, "You really take a lot out of a man." But his tone was one of satisfaction and self-content.

"How do you mean?"

"I'll explain later."

"You must know that you've used up the entire day. I was supposed to work."

"I've only used up the lunchtime part."

"My God! We're supposed to go to the game tonight!"

"Maybe it'll rain."

It did, but not enough. They had supper and while she got it ready, he pinned the horror pictures on a large cardboard. As he ate, he studied them. "You really know the real me."

"You're a monster?" she gasped.

"That's how you make me feel when you're with another man."

"You know full well that I have never 'been with' another man."

"I mean laughing and talking to one."

"Don't ever be jealous. You have no cause."

He swung his head around to look at her full in the face. "Do you mean that?"

"Yes. Nothing could ever make me really angry with you. When you know me better, you'll understand that."

"You've given me some idea of how angry you can get." He indicated the board of horrors. "But I do know you. I've been on your tail ever since you moved in."

"That sounds a little vulgar."

"It wasn't as vulgar as it was—" But she didn't know about that. About how Salty had hired him to watch over her. He completed his sentence. "—interest."

"So you were interested in me from the beginning?"

"As soon as I saw you. But you wouldn't give me the time of day. It took a bargain with Thelma so she would tell you I was keeping track of her, that you finally called on me to help you."

"When Ready first came here—"

"That time you screamed I almost had a heart attack. It never occurred to me that you might actually need help. I was willing to give it anytime, but when you screamed, I thought you might be hurt. I ran down the stairs, having a panic attack. You took forever opening that door. I was about to knock it down. Have you ever noticed those doors are thick and invulnerable? I'd have been more battered than the door."

"That was when the mouse got loose from Felix and hid in the sofa pillows. It was only that."

He nodded. "I aged until I found out." Then he added, "I think Ready and Megen are just right for each other."

"They'll be so relieved to hear you say so."

"Don't get sassy."

"When we were at Tony's, Megen was eyeing you."

"Really?" Tim grinned. "I didn't notice."

"Bah! You noticed. You notice everything. No wonder you're a cop. How long is your leave?"

"I've taken a sabbatical to see if I can write."

"Oh."

"I'm a detective. That's more mental than physical."

"You were very physical with—"

"You're not a criminal."

"—those two men who jumped us that night."

He corrected her. "They accosted us."

"Oh. I hadn't realized the nuance."

"That's why I'm a detective."

"Since you're so mental and aware of nuance, what shall I choose to show at the Art Institute?"

"As much as I hate it, you're right. You need to have one of Ready. You really catch the action in a very knowledgeable way. I'm impressed a woman would draw an athlete as strongly as you can."

She mentioned, "Women are athletes."

He ignored that. "And I think you should have one of the barn cat, Felix. You called Megen's attention to the similarity between Ready and Felix, and it is there. It's very interesting."

"And the third? How about the sea storm?"

"It's great, but as a contrast, what about one of the horrors?"

She guessed narrow-eyed. "You want a picture of yourself in the show if there's one of Ready. You're competitive."

And he laughed.

"You are such a delight," she said to Tim. "I can hardly wait until I can take you home to meet my folks. How about Labor Day? We have a ball game and picnic. There's a water fight, and you'll be exhausted."

"Where would I sleep?"

"Some place discreet."

"No trundling?"

"None."

"You have narrow-minded parents."

"You'll love them."

He did. Now, how was he going to tell her he knew them very well? Since he hadn't mentioned he knew the Browns, how would she take the knowledge?

The Illinois weather continued muggy, hot and growing corn. It looked as though the Cubs would be in the play-offs and every fan was sure that year was the year for the pennant. That was no different. It was their expectation every year.

And Ready was spectacular. He'd been taken up by the press, and he gave shy interviews and discounted the fact he was a brilliant player. He said it was all The Team. The Cubs.

Ready asked if the reporters had seen one play or another? Had they noticed the skill it had taken one or another of the other players? He was earnest and sincere, and he charmed the public. He shared the spotlight. He didn't swagger or strut. But he played ball with all his heart.

The new lovers sat with Megen alongside Ready's family, and they cheered and jumped up and waved their arms and yelled and stayed to the last gasp.

One game went fourteen innings. On into the night, it stayed close, tied two and two. Neither team could make a run. They'd get a man on base, but at the last minute there was a fly ball caught or a reckless dash that was thwarted.

As the overtime innings passed, the earnest fans had drifted down and were standing like gathered water on a tilted pan. They were calling and cheering. And in the middle of the fourteenth inning, with the score still tied at two runs each, the fans began to call for Harry Carey. Then they began to count—a-one, a-two—and wavering, building in volume, the fans began to sing "Take Me Out to the Ball Game." It was very touching.

And in the bottom of that fourteenth inning, the Cubs made a home run.

So the next afternoon, as the team played and the middle of the seventh inning came, Harry Carey called, "Let's hear it now. Help me make up for not being here last night for the fourteenth inning! A-one, a-two—" And they all sang.

# Eight

It was a day or so before Ready had some time off. He came over and said to Carol, "You're a fine woman."

"Why, thank you." But Carol was a little uneasy. She didn't know why Ready was there, and she didn't want any awkward confrontation. She asked, "Want your cat back?"

"If I took him back to the farm, he's the kind to find his way back to Phoebe. Probably in a snowstorm, yowling on your front stoop."

"That's probably true."

"What's true?" Tim came into her apartment. He'd heard their voices and recognized Ready's voice. He'd come down the stairs so fast that he was a little breathless. He looked from one to the other. "Something up?"

"Felix is my cat." Carol sighed deeply.

Tim was surprised. "You just figured that out?"

"There was always a glimmer of hope that Felix would go back to Indiana."

The two men exchanged an amused look.

Then Ready took a breath and began again. He was determined to get it said. He looked at Carol seriously. "I'm in love with Megen."

"We know." It was Tim who responded.

Ready glanced over at Tim, but he looked back at Carol and said kindly, "I wish I could have two wives."

He was being so careful of her that she didn't want to be unkind. She said, "It's okay."

But Tim wouldn't turn it loose. He assured Ready, "I've spoken for this one."

"Well, great! I won't have to worry about her." And he shook hands with Tim in great good humor. "I'll go get Megen and—"

Tim said, "We've got plans."

"What're you going to do? We'll go with you."

Tim shook his head.

Ready stared, considering, working it out. "You want to have her to yourself."

"Yeah."

"Oh. We'll bring supper."

Tim looked at Carol. "Okay?"

She considered Tim. He'd just taken over her life. He was directing what they did and who they saw. She said, "All right." She was giving consent for that particular decision. She continued to look at her man as Ready said his goodbyes and left.

She thought Tim was as much a barn cat as Felix and Ready were. She gave an impatient sigh and frowned.

"You're hurt? You still have feelings for him?" Tim came to her with careful concern.

She realized he wasn't jealous. He didn't need to be. But he was compassionate. It was a surprise. He could be that sure of her, yet he could understand if she had residual feelings for Ready? The thought was really amazing.

She said, "I—I really am pleased for Megen and Ready. She has adored him all along."

He thought Carol was being careful of his feelings and that she did have a nostalgic feeling for Ready. And he said, "I'll bend him for you."

She laughed. "No need. I never did covet Ready. He was just interesting to draw. And he's really a ball player." Then she sobered and stared at Tim. "'Bend' him?"

"Yeah."

"That's what my dad always says if one of us kids is disappointed or being mistreated."

In a crowding spill of words, Tim said, "My dad said the same thing. Your dad was Navy?"

"Yes! I wonder if they knew each other?"

Tim said, "Yeah."

"It would be interesting if they did. It's a small world."

Tim let it go. But his conscience began to gnaw at him.

As sweet as Carol's body was against him, as precious as her kisses were to his heart, Tim knew the time would come when he would have to admit he knew her parents, Salty and Felicia. And he would have to admit to Carol that her father had hired him to guard her.

When she realized Salty had been in the scam, she'd be mad at them both. She'd be annoyed at Salty for not believing she could live safely on her own in the big city.

And she'd be furious with Tim for not being truthful with her.

Tim knew he would have to think of ways around such a confrontation. While he could avoid going with her to Temple, Ohio, someday she might want to show their children to their grandparents.

Tim speculated that when they arrived in Temple, Ohio, and the Brown residence, he could say, "Oh, THAT Salty and Felicia."

Carol would never believe it.

He really began to sweat. He finally figured he'd entrap her so completely that she'd indicate Salty and Felicia with an indecisive hand and say, "These are my—uh—parents? I call them...uh...Mom and Dad."

How does one entrap a woman and write a book at the same time? He put his book aside during the day and wrote at night. His book was becoming steamy, like the weather. Or like hot sex.

In a flurry of activity and insecurity, Carol became prolific. She painted a skyline oil of Chicago. It was beautifully done, but it had been multitudinously done.

She put it aside rather nostalgically.

Tim said, "We'll hang it in the hall when we move to Arizona."

She straightened and pinned him with a look. "Arizona?"

He shrugged. "Spokane?"

"Why would we leave Chicago?"

So she had admitted that where he would go, she would go. The knowledge comforted Tim.

He mentioned to her, "You have a couple of months to sort out what you want to show at the Institute. You don't have to work so hard. You could give me a little attention."

"You've already had your attention for today."

"I need you to sit on my lap and flirt with me."

She turned her head and looked him over with shrewd and smugly blatant evaluation and with a little smile. "There. I've flirted with you." And she went back to work.

He huffed and puffed. Then he laughed. But he complained, "You didn't sit on my lap."

Carrying her palette on one hand and big brush in the other, she went to him to perch on his knees for a careful minute. "There." Her tone was one of accomplishment. She went back to her easel.

He was indignant.

He went over to her and removed the palette and brush from her hands, and he kissed her.

Then he picked her up and carried her to the bedroom, shooed the cats away and closed the door against their reentry.

But Tim didn't strip her as she expected. He lay down beside her and asked, "What's your first memory?"

"Let's see." She considered. "I was about three and—"

"Of me."

"Oh."

He prodded, "What'd you think the first time you saw me?"

"You loomed around."

"Loomed?"

"Yes. That's what it seemed like to me. And it is strange because you're not that tall and—"

Indignantly, he chuffed. "I'm six feet tall!"

"But that's not loomingly tall."

"Well, I'm not seven feet ten, but I'm a decent height."

She looked at him with a little smile and agreed. "You're perfect."

"You're shorter than me."

"I—"

"Yeah. You're shorter."

She was kind. "I admit it."

"You act like I'm a runt."

"I never said so."

He accused, "You said I wasn't tall at all."

"You have some problem with height?"

"Well, I just wanted to say I'm big enough for you."

She became a little impatient. "I never said you weren't!"

"Okay, you don't have to argue about it."

"I wasn't!"

"I'm tall enough."

She confirmed. "Six feet."

"Actually... it's five eleven."

She licked her smile, but it wouldn't go away. She looked over at him, her eyes brimming humor. He was looking at the ceiling.

He asked, "Did you notice anything, beside me looming?"

So she settled down to talk to him about him. "Let's see. How do I tell you this? Do you understand that women don't actually look at men unless they feel very safe? Looking right at men is a lot like looking at a strange dog. Dogs get hostile, growl and attack. Men take a woman looking at them as an invitation to tangle."

"Phooey."

"Yes."

"So. When you finally looked at me, what did you see?"

"When I actually looked at you, I saw a man who could be dangerous. You scared me a little."

"I was protecting you!" He blurted the words before he knew what he was saying.

But she didn't assimilate his meaning right then. She was remembering. She had her chin up and her eyes slitted as she looked out the window. "You could have been The Strangler."

He sat up. "My God, woman, that's a terrible thing to say!"

"You asked!"

"I want to hear you say that you got all hot and heavy breathing over me, and you tell me I looked like a strangler? How can you be so dumb?"

She lay silently. He sat in indignation. She moved to sit up, but she looked at him and realized he was offended. She said, "You're very good-looking. I love your rifted eyebrow."

He lay back down. "You drew horror pictures of me."

"I was angry."

"I'm a good man."

"I know that." She smiled a little. "This is a silly conversation."

"It might be to you."

"I offended you when you asked me what I saw when I first knew you, and I was honest. Women have to assume that men are not simply facades. Women need to be cautious. Women alone can't always trust lone men."

"That's true."

"I knew nothing about you."

"I loomed." He was disgruntled.

"But you didn't molest me. You were careful of me. Then Thelma said I should call on you if I needed someone. I did. I remember all the times you came down those stairs immediately. You've been my guardian angel."

There was a silence. Then he said, "I'm your love." His voice was roughened and tender.

"That, too."

He licked his lips and asked gently, "When did you know you loved me?"

She replied without hesitation, "When Ready kissed me."

He leaned back his head and exclaimed, "God Almighty!" He was disgusted.

"Well . . . you asked!"

"You hadn't known before then?"

She began to get terse. "No. I had not!" And she enunciated the words in some hostility.

"You said the sky didn't fall when he kissed you. Have I made the sky fall for you?"

Sitting there beside him she watched him for a minute. He was lying flat, his head on her pillow. He looked good there. Softly, she said, "No."

His eyes so sad, he moved his head to look at her. He didn't say anything.

"There's no comparison between you and Ready."

But he misunderstood. He sighed sadly. "Yeah. He's about the best baseball player there is."

She told him tartly, "When you kissed me, you tilted the universe—" She heard him take a quick, surprised breath. She added soberly, "Planets changed places."

"For you, too?" He grinned at her.

"God only knows what all havoc you wreaked just by kissing me. Have you gone around kissing other women that way? Are they all dead from you exploding their brains? Wrecking their breathing systems? Addling their thinking?''

"All that?"

"Yes." She was a bit hostile.

He became conciliatory. "I felt it, too, you know."

She wasn't lured. She stated it practically, "You had to because you were a part of it all."

"We shared it."

"We were both boggled by something unusual. That isn't love. That's only sensation."

He raised up on one elbow. "Are you claiming we're not in love?"

"I'll have to reconsider."

"Why?"

"I had no idea you have a height problem."

"No, not me. It's you that's so paranoid that you think every man around is panting to jump your bones."

"So?"

He lay back and sighed. "You're probably right." He moved a little impatiently, shifting. Then he said, "Any man would try for you." But he hadn't said it to flatter her, his voice was sour.

"And women avoid you?"

"You sure as hell did."

"I called on you to save me."

"That's just convenience."

"I didn't call on any of the other guys who live in this house."

"You can't trust them," he agreed. Then he asked in some consternation, "You considered me harmless?"

She countered, "I invited you to kiss me."

"When was that?"

"When the sky didn't fall in with Ready. I was willing to see if it would with you."

"I'm not sure that's flattering."

"You declined."

"I was smelly and sweaty and pretty ripe. I don't wash my jogging clothes very often."

She guessed: "The smell repels hostile dogs?"

"Yeah. But it could revolt a delicate lady like you. I didn't want to revolt you or make you gag."

"I didn't."

"You could give me a little kiss now. Nothing earth-shaking or anything, but just a little one so my morale doesn't falter."

"Your morale is . . . faltering?"

"I'm expanding my vocabulary. I'm a writer now. While an artist can paint the same picture over and over under different lights, a writer can't keep using the same words. You should kiss me before I go into a decline."

"It's that serious?"

"Yeah."

She leaned over him, not touching his chest with her soft breasts, and she kissed him gently. Only their lips touched.

She lifted her head, watching him.

He opened his eyes and said, "You're careful not to touch me. You scared of me?"

"Every time I get on this bed with you, something remarkable and exhausting happens to me."

"What's that?"

"You."

He demurred. "You like me fooling around with you."

"It was interesting, but it's a lot like words. It's just the same old thing."

"You challenging me?" He raised himself up onto one elbow.

"Not at all."

He moved over, sitting up and pushing her backward with his chest. "I feel challenged."

Flat on her back, she challenged, "You've used that word twice, now."

"Be quiet."

"Are you ordering me around?"

"No. I just told you to be quiet."

"Why—"

And he kissed her. It was the planet-switching kind. He lifted his mouth and looked at his victim.

She considered carefully, "I did have some brains left."

"You realize that I'm superior?"

"What brains I have left are scrambled."

"I thought it was the planets that were whirled around."

"No. I can't think." She put the back of her hand to her head with her curled, helpless fingers outward.

"Good. I'll do your thinking for you. Undress."

"I thought we used your last condom."

"I have a spare, just in case. Here. Let me help with the buttons."

"I'm capable of buttons."

"Then I didn't scramble you enough." And he kissed her again, moving his hands around and making her wiggle and squirm to get closer to him, to get more. He lifted his mouth to tell her, "You're really very shocking, Miss Brown." His voice was trembly and guttural.

The contrast between his formal words and his primitive voice was delightful to her. She wiggled a little more. She pushed him flat onto his back and leaned over him.

"You're getting salacious, Miss Brown. No, no. Not there. Why, Miss Brown! Does your mother know you do that kind of thing? Over a little farther. There. Oh, Miss Brown, you are a flirt!"

She lifted her mouth. "Flirt? You call this... flirting?"

"I don't know the proper word."

"What's the improper one?"

"Uhhhh. I'd better not mention it."

She gasped, "Do you mean there IS a word?"

"Well, yeah. Go on. Do it again."

She coaxed, "Tell me the word, first."

"I'm not sure I remember it clearly. Do it again while I try to think. If you're doing it, maybe I can remember what it's called."

She laughed low and lecherously.

He whimpered a little but moved so that she wouldn't hurt her neck.

She lifted her head and gave him a quizzical look. "Has anyone else seduced you?"

"Not that I can recall."

"You'd recall."

"Well, you kissed me a minute ago, and my brains were scrambled."

She corrected, "It was mine that were scrambled."

"Something happened to me, too."

"It will. I'm in control. You're the victim."

In a tiny voice he tried to pitch high, he whispered, "Help, help."

She laughed and blew air onto him with her mouth close to his skin.

In a strained voice, he urged, "I hope you realize just what you're doing to me?"

"I'm trying to attract your attention."

He laughed at something so ridiculous. He curled up enough to put his hands under her arms and dragged her up him. "Now it gets serious."

But it didn't. She played and teased and wiggled and tickled, and it was a whole different kind of loving. At one point she almost slid off the side of the bed and she had to squeal and ask for help. His strong arm held her balanced, and he made her plead.

"I'll promise anything!" she gasped, faking terror at a scant two-foot drop to a soft carpet. She acted as if she were dangling over an abyss.

"Anything?"

"Yes/yes/yes! Save me! Save me!"

"Marry me."

"Good grief, Timothy Bolt. No man proposes to a woman who's dangling off the side of her very own bed. That's coercion."

"Then I can drop you?"

"I wouldn't advise you to do that."

He smiled a very little bit and pretended to do just that, and as he allowed her to slip about two inches, she shrieked.

He scolded, "Carol!"

"Nobody ever hears me yell. Only you."

"I can see Thelma running to my room for help and, not finding me there, calling the police."

In a whisper, she said, "Help! Help!"

With an awesome display of muscle power, holding her weight with one arm and not allowing her to slip farther, he moved his body over to the edge and kissed her sassy mouth.

She gave a naughty chuckle.

"You want to be rescued?"

"If you pull me back up on that bed, are you going to let me go, unassaulted?"

"No."

"Then what sort of 'rescue' did you have in mind?"

"You can either come up here and cooperate with the consequences, or you can slide on down to the floor and submit there."

"Is this what they mean about out of the frying pan and into the fire?"

"I'm not sure, but you sure make me hot. Want to feel me?"

"Sir! That's a lewd invitation."

"Why, Carol! All's I meant was for you to put your hand on my forehead. What did you think I meant?"

She could only laugh. It was a low chuckle and extremely naughty.

"That does it. You've convinced me!" He began to pull her back up onto the bed.

"What?" She looked around in little head jerks, saying, "What'd I say? What'd I convince you about? Help/Help/Help! What are you doing? You carnal-minded man. You lustful, bestial, ruttish goat."

And he gathered her under him and said, "Yeah."

They were as intimate as two people of the opposite sex could be, when there came a great, reverberating pounding on her apartment door.

Tim collapsed on top of Carol and growled. "Your scream." And the tone was accepting.

"Don't be sil—"

A door-filtered, deep Thelma voice called, "Carol! Carol!"

Carol wiggled out from under Tim and called, "Just a minute! I'm coming."

Tim growled, "I wish."

She braced her hand on his face and got out of bed.

He said, "How can you move that way?"

"Hush." She snatched up the brazen kimono her mother had given her that was of perfect colors, and she said needlessly, "Stay here. I'll handle this."

"Hurry it up."

"Good grief," she said in some disgust. And she closed the bedroom door as she went out.

She opened the big door to her apartment and asked, "What's up?"

There was Thelma with two policemen, some of the grad students from the attic and the poet.

They looked at her whisker-burned face, her hand-smoothed hair and the intemperate kimono, and they were speechless.

She asked, "Is there a problem?"

And the cops asked, "Are you a prisoner?"

"Of course not."

The poet asked, "May we check?"

"You may. Just you. I don't want anyone else in my place right now."

They all stood around while the poet went in and looked through the apartment.

Thelma said, "I heard you scream?"

"Why, it must have been the mouse, but Felix caught it and—" she shivered delicately "—ate it." She said, "You were—ahhh. How kind of you, to be sure. Thank you, very much. I am sorry. But the mouse surprised me." She explained to the two cops. "We've almost gotten rid of them all."

Felix came down from one of her drafting tables, and as he walked over to the group by the door, he said something.

Carol was just glad the cops and the students and Thelma couldn't understand the damned cat because from his tone, it was very obvious he was altering her story.

The poet came back to the living room area and said, "All's well. I did find a mouse tail. Otherwise, there are no surprises." He gave Carol a bland look.

She didn't offer coffee or anything else. She said, "You must excuse me. You caught me at an awkward minute." The poet choked rather gently. She gave him a mild look and patted his back. "Thank you for checking up on me. I really do appreciate it."

"You're welcome."

She closed the door slowly, listening to Thelma explaining the scream she'd heard, excusing herself for calling the police.

But the cops said, "Always call. Never decide it's not worth investigating. We'd rather see a woman who is tousled by some playing man than go too late and find one dead."

She went back to the bedroom and found Tim with the sheet up to his chin. She said, "It happened just the way you said it would. Do you know how many times I've screamed in my life and no one has come to check?"

"I did."

"I mean before you."

"They were nice to come. I'll tell them."

"You'll shoot my reputation all to hell."

"They already know about us."

"How could they possibly?"

"I told them to watch out for this house. You and Thelma are the only ladies here. They would eliminate Thelma. They came because I told them about you. They did it for you. They do that for anyone. But they did this one for you."

"I'll take them a cake."

"They'd like it." Then he asked, "Why did you let the poet check out the apartment instead of one of the cops?"

"I didn't know you didn't mind the cops knowing you were playing around with me."

"Allowing the poet into the apartment and not the cops, they already know what was going on."

"No."

"Cops know people."

"The poet likes men."

"He's loyal to the man he lives with. They've been together a long time."

"Why? Did you try for him?"

Tim was patient. "I checked out everyone in this house."

"Why? Did you think some old enemy of yours would be here for revenge?"

"I wanted to be sure this was a safe house when you moved in down here."

That was the truth. He'd told her the real reason. If ever she accused him of lying to her, he could tell her that.

She undid the intemperate kimono and opened it up. She glanced up at him and saw she had his attention. She shimmied a little as she appeared to have trouble with those big sleeves, and he watched that also, his face sober.

She put the kimono on the chair by the door and approached the bed in careful steps. He was riveted. She said, "Where were we?"

"You were on the bottom."

"How can you remember?"

"I had my toes dug into the bed."

Again she asked, "How do you remember that?"

"I was trying to keep you from bucking me off."

"You are a libertine."

"Yeah."

"Well, I've cooled down considerably. Having Thelma and the police and all those other people catch me in the middle of an illicit romp has embarrassed me considerably."

"Why?"

"Well, I'm not that kind of person."

"Yes, you are. Come here."

So she climbed back into bed with him.

Then they had to gather up the cats and put them out into the hall. Carol said, "I don't know why we insist they not be with us. They already know all about sex."

"I'm afraid one will get in the way, and I'll squash it and that would distract you."

She agreed. "I can see that."

"Where were we?"

"I was on the bottom."

His voice was smoky as he told her, "Come here."

She wiggled and squirmed to get under him in the limited space he'd left for her. "It seems so blatant for me to just get into bed and get under you this way. No romance. Mechanical." She said the words between his kisses.

"You want romance?"

"Yep."

"You should say, 'Please, darling.'"

"Please, darling."

So he romanced her right out of her mind and into paradise. He did it with finesse. With skill.

She gasped, "How did you know to do that?"

"You showed me."

"When?"

"The first time I kissed you."

"In my studio? I'd have never done that out there in front of all those windows."

"Yep."

"Oh, that is lovely."

"How about . . . this."

"Ohhhh, yeeessssss."

Outside of the police coming, it was a lovely afternoon.

# Nine

----

When Phoebe had her kittens, it was in the middle of the night. It was the tiny squeakings which wakened Carol. Phoebe purred the entire time. How did she know to do that?

Felix lay aside, listening, alert, watching. Guarding. He made Caruso stay away. Once he spat and swiped at the curious younger cat.

Carol called Tim. "Tim, guess what—"

"What's the matter? I'll be right down." And he hung up.

She had her door open before he could pound on it at such an hour. She held up a finger to her lips and said, "Shhhh. Phoebe is having her kittens."

Tim was in his robe. Tousle-headed. And Carol smoothed his hair and kissed him. They phoned Megen and Ready.

Megen wasn't terribly interested, but Ready came over and watched. Felix allowed Ready to scratch his head and brag on him. Ready told the other humans, "Our barn cats never let us know until the mother brought them out. We'd know they were somewhere, the mother was skinny again, but the cats hid the kittens."

With daylight, the news spread throughout the house. It was interesting, the possessiveness that the inhabitants of the building showed. Felix had been an important introduction into a mouse-beleaguered house.

They decided no stranger should have any of the six kittens. They put in thoughtful bids on the kittens, discussing them and arguing. To no one's surprise, the kittens were named and owned before they ever opened their eyes.

All the while the house's distractions persisted, Chicago went on, busy and involved and quarreling and having events which the inhabitants attended and talked about. The Cubs were in the play-offs. As usual, the fans knew this was a Cubs year. No question about it. But then, it was *always* a Cubs year.

Megen traveled to the games out of town, and sometimes Carol went with her.

Once Tim asked, "Do you go for Megen or for Ready?"

Carol gave him an extremely tolerant look and said, "Naturally, I go along for the sake of . . . Ready."

"Oh."

"You idiot."

"I'm jealous. I'm possessive. I'm a territorial male."

"Come along next time."

"I write like hell while you're gone and not distracting me."

Thoughtfully, she undid her blouse. "I distract you?"

"You tease."

She looked up, all wide-eyed innocence. "I'm a tease? Why?"

"Undoing your shirt that way."

"It's a blouse and there's no other way to undo it. I can't take it off over my head, it has to be unbuttoned. I don't see why you think I'm a tease." She looked so innocent.

He narrowed his eyes and growled, "Undoing your blouse that way."

"There's paint on it. I have to change." She clasped it together at her throat. "I hadn't realized I was exposing myself to a susceptible male."

"I'm not susceptible. I'm an observer of moral behavior. I can't be anything else, right now. You've got me so limp, I'll never be able to rise to another occasion."

Carol burst into giggles.

But having rebuttoned the paint-dotted shirt, she showed Tim her sketchbook. "This is what I was doing at the last game out east."

She'd done crowd sketches, people cheering, men giving indifferent umpires hell, women laughing, spectators scrambling for a foul ball. It was all there. And there were sketches of the players. Even some of Ready.

She explained how she took lead pencils of various softness. With those, she took colored pencils of yellow, blue and red and used those basic ones to make all the colors. Her grey pencil accents to blobs of color for the distant, crowded stands made the viewer's mind see people there as real.

She told Tim, "One of the interesting things to do in looking at a crowd is teaching your eyes to register only one color. If you think red and look at a crowd, it seems the majority of people are in red. Then do that with blue or yellow or green. It's entertaining."

Thoughtfully, she said, "People apply a selective process to everything. Like those who see or hear only humor or only evil...."

"I learned to see selective colors while I was watching football at school. Sitting so high in the stadium, the players down on the field were little sticks flying around and piling up on a distant spot. I didn't enjoy football until I watched it on TV. With the replays and the accounting, the game is interesting—unless you get some Chatty Charlie who doesn't know when to shut up."

"You like sports."

"One...especially."

"Which?" Tim watched her.

She removed the blouse and she did show him. Afterward, she asked, "Are all men such slow learners?"

"Now, how would I know that?"

"We always have to do the same old thing over and over and over."

"I'll read ahead," he promised. In the following days, he introduced her to doing it in a chair, on the floor and against the wall. The chair was a challenge, the floor was hard, and the bathroom tiles were cold. But she hadn't noticed until afterward.

Tim invited her on a picnic and wouldn't allow her to bring anything. They drove forever, getting out of the city to the west.

She said, "This has been fascinating. We could have gone to any Chicago park and had a picnic there or along the lakeshore."

He replied courteously, "This is so you can do it in the back seat of the car."

"Alone? How will I manage?"

So he showed her.

At an emotionally riveted period of their experiment, a horse came along and tried to put its head through the window, and Carol shrieked.

Tim hit his head on the ceiling light and tangled his foot in his drawers.

The sober-faced horse bolted only a short distance before it stopped and looked back.

And only cats are considered curious?

It took a quick look around to know they were still alone, and it was a couple of minutes after that when they started to laugh.

But they went back to her apartment and made love on her bed.

During that part of the summer, Carol had made several trips home for quick visits. It wasn't far. She coaxed Tim, "Come with me. I'd like my folks to meet you."

"We'll do it another time. I'm getting to a crucial part of my book, and I have to pay attention. I work better when you're not around distracting me."

She couldn't see how she could possibly distract him. So he had to show her. Her surprise was almost believable.

At home in Temple, Ohio, Carol showed Felicia the drawings and watercolors that she was considering for the show at the Art Institute. Felicia said they were all perfect.

Salty agreed and asked, "Who's the ball player? Looks like Ready Farthington."

"Actually, it is."

"You know him?"

"His bat broke and hit my leg last spring."

"You never mentioned it."

"It wasn't anything. But he started coming over, and he met Megen. Remember her?"

"She's from school, isn't she?" Felicia inquired.

"You remember her from then?"

Felicia laughed her marvelous low chuckle and said, "I didn't think you cared much for her."

"She's changed." And she told her parents about Megen's love for Ready Farthington.

"He can probably handle Megen," Felicia decided.

"Yes." Carol then told the family about Felix the cat, and the older ones groaned and the younger ones exclaimed, "Ready? You've met READY FARTHINGTON?" Her stock went up some sixty points.

She showed Saul, Ben, Jake and Teller her watercolors of Ready, and for the second or third time since they'd known Carol, they were impressed. The first time had been when she'd thrown an almost impossible shot with a basketball and it had swished through.

They were still young. They still had time to learn women are superior.

Salty asked about the people in the house, and if they were all behaving properly?

Carol blushed and said they were a great, friendly bunch.

Salty asked his daughter, "Anybody hustling you?"

"No. Not especially." She blushed scarlet and looked casual.

So Salty called Tim and asked, "Anybody hustling Carol?"

Tim replied with slow seriousness, not knowing what Carol might have said to them. "Hustling her? Not that

I know. I'm around her enough, I'd know if somebody was."

And Salty smiled at the telephone.

So Carol went back to Chicago and to Timothy Bolt. They were exuberant to see each other again after the eternal parting of two days. They went right to bed. And they did have the bed to themselves.

Tim had moved the cats into a bottom compartment of Carol's window-side cabinet. Caruso had the next one over. Felix had wherever he wanted. Being the barn cat he was, he shifted his sleeping place rather frequently. He especially liked the top of the cabinets.

Since Carol liked the tops of the cabinets for drying watercolors, and cat hair and toe jam weren't conducive to a pristine watercolor, a table had to be moved so the barn cat couldn't get that vital leg up to the top of the cabinet. He was still trying.

Not any lover of cats, even though Carol said he, too, was a barn cat, Tim did explain Felix to Carol, "You can see any king of the jungle needing to be up far enough to take control over everything."

But her reply left no hope. "No."

"Are you planning on limiting me?"

She was surprised. "You want to sleep on the tops of the cabinets?"

"No."

"Then I see no problem."

Tim knew there was one, she just didn't yet know about it. He told her, "I've finished my book."

"When can I read it."

"Now."

"Will it terrify me?"

"I fervently hope so."

"I'm not sure I can read it. I do get scared."

"I'll give up sleeping on the tops of the cabinets and sleep with you."

She complained, "I'd never get to sleep."

"I don't snore . . . really bad."

"How do you know? Who's slept with you and reported on how you snore?"

He gasped in shock at the idea and opened out his hands, he was so vulnerable, and he said defensively, "I've only wakened myself a couple of times."

"You're probably the buzz saw type."

"I grew up at my grandmother's, and she told me I had a comforting snore, just like my dad's."

"The sailor? He probably wasn't home enough for her to be critical."

"My grandmother was a picky woman."

"Was?"

"Yeah. They're both gone. She died some time ago, but my dad died just a couple of years ago."

"Your mother?"

"She took off when I was little."

"Ahhh." Then she said, "You must have really loved your dad and grandmother to miss them so much."

"I'll miss them all of my life. I wish they could have known you and seen our kids and compared them with others in the family. Our kids will have everybody's faults."

"Those will be balanced by my sterling characteristics."

"You have some?"

"You beast."

"I am, you know." In dead seriousness, he asked, "What if you discovered I'd lied to you?"

"Why would you do that?" She studied him in the silence. Then she told him, "If you did lie, you would have had a good reason. It wouldn't be about anything important to me or to my well-being.'' Then she asked, ''Have you?''

And he lied. ''No.''

''Did you say all that to get me into the right frame of mind to read your book?''

''No.''

''I wonder if I should read it. I'm not a horror fan. If it frightens me, I could discourage you.''

''The poet has a copy.''

''Him?'' Carol was surprised.

Tim corrected the word. ''He.''

She thought Tim was just reiterating the identity, so she confirmed it. ''He.''

''Yep.''

She was amazed the poet would like horror stories. Poetry and horror didn't appear to have anything in common. ''Well, I'll be darned. Why him?''

''He's very sensitive. He loves words, and he's a horror freak.''

''I'm almost afraid to read your book.''

''Then don't.''

She was exasperated. ''I'm too curious not to.''

''Then read it.''

''You're no help at all.''

He droned ponderously, ''I'm helpful to you in many ways.''

''Oh, yes? Tell me.''

''I take care of you.''

''And?''

He questioned, ''You want more?''

''Of course. If I'm to judge you, then I have to know.''

"Haven't you already made up your mind about me? Or are you still trying me out and judging me?"

"I suppose I'll be trying you out all the rest of our lives."

He smiled. It was slow and gradual, but his face became a beam of delight. "You love me."

"Perhaps."

"No *perhaps* about it. You love me."

She sighed gustily. "I suppose."

"How can you tell?"

"The two days I was at home were ten years long. I missed you so badly. I kept looking for you and listening for you. I wanted you to see my young adopted brothers, Saul and Ben, Jake and Teller. And the two little girls who are both seven now. They are all such nice kids. Did you miss me a little?"

"Yeah, I guess so."

"You GUESS so! Why, you—"

She attacked him, and he put her over his shoulder and took her back to bed.

When she could talk, she said, "Sex is your side of the argument."

"What argument?"

"Whether or not you love me."

"I told you once. How many times do you have to hear it?"

"Every breath, or at least once a day."

"I'll put it on my schedule."

"UUUHHHH! Men!"

And he laughed.

"Tell me you missed me while I was home."

"I missed you while you were home."

"That isn't sincere."

"I said what you wanted to hear and what I wanted you to hear. I love you. You scare the hell out of me, you are so perfect. I can't bear to have you out of my sight. I'm so afraid some hero is going to catch your eye . . . and I'll die if I'm discarded."

She was stunned. "You feel all that?"

"Yeah." He started to get out of bed.

She stopped him and hugged him.

He said, "Damn you. You've got me caught so tight in your web that I'll be underfoot all your life, just hoping you are too distracted to see I'm only a man."

"Only?" Her eyes were filmed with tears. "Oh, Timothy, darling. You are so special. How could I have ever found you? I moved in here, and you were just upstairs. It was a miracle." She put her head on his back and hugged him to her.

He thought the miracle was named Salty. When would she know? Why had Salty commanded that she not be told? Why the secrecy?

Tim's soul writhed in the deception. Could he have time enough so that she would know him well enough for them to survive her knowing that her father had set them up to meet and fall in love?

What could Tim say? *Your dad paid me to look after you?* She'd react like any other smugly independent woman who thought she'd managed on her own.

But she would have.

Look at the people who lived in the house— Yeah? Look at them! Grad students. A male couple. A woman of the theater. A strange mix. Had they been selected by Salty . . . too? Was Thelma a long-time cohort of Felicia's?

It would be just like those two to contrive this whole setup. And without really thinking about it, he thought of the cabinets that had already been put in place. When Carol had seen them, she had gasped in delight. Who'd put those there? And Tim knew he'd known all along. It had been Salty.

But Salty *had* admitted to having the windows strengthened and wired. He'd admitted doing that. Then Tim thought to himself: Come on, Tim, you're seeing ghosts. Just because Salty hired you, doesn't mean he had any grand scheme. If he installed the cabinets, it was because he knew what Carol would need in her work. She probably already knows he did that.

Tim asked Carol, "The cabinets. How did you get them?"

"They were here—"

"Yeah."

"My dad had them installed. He'd found them in a friend's studio when it was being dismantled. He found them several years ago and put them in storage. Dad was sorry they didn't go clear to the ceiling."

"But you like them that height."

"I told him that last weekend. He was so pleased."

"Did you show them the horror pictures you did of me?"

"Two."

"Did they know you painted them because of me?"

"No. I decided not to mention I have a housemate who is a horror. It might rattle them."

"When did you know about the cabinets?"

"When he found them. He took me to see them. He wanted to be sure they were what I would want."

See? If Salty had set his daughter up for some man, even if the man was his good friend's son, he would have had them meet first. The arrangement that had seemed contrived had been completely innocent.

Mentally, Tim apologized to the man who had been responsible for helping him have the time to write this first book...and to know Carol. Bringing the two of them together hadn't been a setup. While Salty had been thinking of Carol's safety, he'd also thought to help his friend's son with the time to write.

After supper, Carol began to read the book. It began: "For an isolated place, it was in a reasonable location. The house was up on a hill, so it got the cooling winds...."

She groused, "So it's isolated. How nasty of you to point that out first thing."

"I'm just setting the scene."

"Yeah, and I know what's going to happen. They won't be able to get any help. The phone goes out right after the lights."

He laughed.

"You have a very dirty laugh. It's smug."

She settled down and read. She started shifting in jerks. She glared at him. She read, furiously turning the pages...and she forgot about him. That made him hold his breath. If she could forget he was there and watching her, wouldn't it mean the story had caught her attention?

He put a glass of water on the table by her. She automatically drank of it. And she read. She finished it four hours later, and she was groggy. She looked at him for some time. Then she said, "I hate you. How could you do this to me?"

"What?"

"You've scared me spitless."

"Good." He smiled in satisfaction.

"Instead of calling it *The House,* you might think about calling it *Isolation* or *The Lost House* or *The*

*Isolated House.* Give a little clue that this house is different.''

''Good suggestion. Any others?''

''No.'' She shook her head. ''You did a great job of it. My God, how your mind works!''

He smiled wider.

''The publishers will be fighting over you with your third book.''

''Not the first one?''

''Yeah. Whoever gets first choice will be cautious. With the second one, they'll get interested.''

''And the third?''

''That's when some overworked editor will take up a copy of the first one and frown at it and flip through it, and settle down and read it, and miss her stop on the subway and end up God only knows where. Then she'll stagger into the office the next day and demand to see to the top man and tell him, 'Read this!' and history will be made.''

''Then you like the book.''

''It scared the liver out of me.''

He smiled some more. ''You won't want to sleep alone toni—''

''You did this just so I'd sleep with you?''

''Would there be another reason?''

''You're going to be famous. ANY woman will sleep with you.''

''Cowards like you.''

''I am not a coward.''

And seriously, he agreed. ''No, you most certainly are not. You're a remarkable woman.''

''Yes.''

''And modest.''

''Just honest.''

He laughed aloud and got up to stretch.

She watched him do that. "You promised to sleep with me."

"I've slept with you a couple of times today."

"I don't mean you have to have sex with me, you have to guard me from all the ghosts and goblins and things that go bump in the night."

He nodded soberly, considering, and said, "I can do that."

"You have no choice." She was positive. "You *have* to do that."

"Well, darn. Do you suppose I'm going to have to sleep with every female who reads my book?"

"No."

"Well, if I have to for you, wouldn't it only be polite to offer—"

She interrupted: "No."

"Are you possessive, too?"

"Very."

"Ahhhh." He considered. "Maybe you should have told me that earlier, before I got...entangled."

"No."

"Now, why not?"

She was serious. "I might have scared you off."

"Do you know how long I had to work to get you to pay attention to me?"

Disgruntled, she confessed sourly, "I might just as well tell you that I was really rattled the first time I saw you, and I was avoiding you. Artists are open people. I would have liked living openly and in a carefree manner. I didn't want to get this involved at this time."

"And I got you."

She put out her hands, palms up. "For better or worse."

"Worse." He tasted the word thoughtfully. "What about this *worse* that you've only now brought up?"

"You might find out I'm not as pliant as I've been pretending."

"You've hoodwinked me? You're a shrew?"

"I'm not sure. I've never really been on my own and I could well go bonkers."

"Why?"

"You have no idea how confining my parents are about behavior! They are archaic! And at school, it wasn't much better. If you want grades and House respect, you have to work. There isn't the time to dillydally."

"I'm—" He considered her. "I'm just a—dillydally?"

"No. I got caught."

"You're *pregnant?*" Salty would kill him.

"No, silly. My emotions are caught. By you."

"I did mean to do that. But I've been very careful not to catch you in any other way."

"I know."

"When I sleep with you tonight, I won't touch you seriously." He was earnest. "I want you to know I have control."

"I don't. Bring some condoms down, just in case I convince you."

"There's just nothing worse than artists. They're free livers."

"They eat liver?"

"Do you suppose you're going to go on all our lives making puns and indulging your penchant for word play?"

"Penchant?" She lifted her eyebrows.

"That's one of my new words."

"If you think artists are wild and free, I've heard a lot of really serious comments about the loose morals of writers."

He held up his hand like a rookie cop. "Not true."

"How come you've been all over me in my bed?" she inquired.

"That had nothing to do with my writing, that was solely because you were alive and tackled me at a weak moment."

"Do you mean to imply this has all been my fault because I'm an artist? You've been the . . . victim?"

"Yeah."

"Bull."

"Why, Carol Brown! Does your father know you use that word?"

"I doubt it."

And Tim laughed.

"It's late. Go get your pajamas and your entire supply of condoms."

"Horror turns you on?"

"I'll need to be distracted from such a shivery, scary story."

"A man's work is never done."

"Oh, for Pete's sake."

"I'm doing all this for some guy named Pete?"

"Just go do what you're supposed to do."

He stood up and unzipped his shorts.

"Not that. Go get your pajamas and the condoms."

"I sleep naked."

"Glory be."

"I don't believe I have suspected just what I've taken on here. If you're this voracious, I have to be braced for a full night of you. I need my strength."

She guessed: "You're hungry."

"Eating would take up some of the time I'm facing."

"I've never heard of any man putting up such a resistance! I thought men *loved* spending the night with an illicit woman."

He countered, "You're not illicit."

"Well, I can pretend for a little while, before you make me legal."

"Who said I would?"

She protested, "You asked me to marry you."

"Did I sign it?"

"Oh, go home."

"No. You've committed yourself to sleeping with me and you're going to do it."

"Does everyone who does this go through all this chatter?" she asked. "Or do they simply go to bed and sleep?"

"I don't know."

"You're a writer, what would you write?"

"I think I'd have her get into his bed."

"Why."

"Men are victims. Women just make it seem that men are the aggressors so they can pretend to be the victims."

"Wait a minute there, buddy."

"Buddy?" he asked. "We're friends! That's a good start."

She stood up and walked around, holding her head. "You are worth putting up with some quirks. Your humor needs upgrading. We can work on that. Go... upstairs... and get anything you might need."

"I have everything with me."

She looked down his body and a smile crept in, making her mouth curl slightly. "I must say, I have to agree with you. Do you have a toothbrush?"

"At camp, we learned to use our finger."

She accepted that. "I'll show you a choice in toothpaste."

"That's a nice, welcoming gesture."

"Do you want something to eat?"

"Maybe in an hour or so. You forget I've been watching you breathe and shift around in that chair all evening and half the night. I didn't want to interrupt such a good book, but since you don't have anything else to do, I thought we might go to bed and test the springs."

"That again?"

He did some sort of funky step and sang the television commercial from a couple of years back. "Uh-huh, uh-huh, that's the way, you'll like it. Uh-huh, uh-huh."

She said to Phoebe, "I believe you got the better barn cat."

Tim rushed Carol, bent her over his shoulder, went into the bedroom and closed the door on the following cats. He leaned over and dropped her on the bed. "You'll like it."

# Ten

The two lovers laughed and tussled on the bed, just playing. Then they lay quietly, smiling at each other in the dim light. Tim said, "You're the nicest woman I've ever known."

And Carol replied, "Substituting *male* for *woman,* you are superior. I favor you."

He leaned over her and kissed her forehead. "Where's your toothpaste?"

"In the bathroom cabinet."

He considered. "That seems logical enough." He got off the bed and went to the door. "Want the cats inside?"

"Naw. I've found something else to keep me warm."

"I'm even furry."

She lay on the bed, smiling a little, waiting for him to return. When she heard the shower running, she went to join him. He was delighted. He got to wash her, which he did meticulously. She was harder to rinse than he.

And she washed him. She didn't get to do a very good job of it, because he got out of the shower and pulled her out.

They did dry themselves fairly well before they went back to the bed.

In a rather remarkably short time, they dragged from the bed and changed the sheets and mattress pad. She blow-dried her hair. Then they slept. They slept and roused when they ran into each other, turning in their sleep, and there would be the surprise and the smile and touching before they slept again.

And they slept late the next morning. They wakened to yawn and kiss and stretch and smile. And they made sweet and tender love.

Their day was lazy. Carol did sketches of the brilliant new author, and they smiled a whole lot. Any observer would have become impatient with their silly behavior, but no one else was around.

Finally, Tim went up and wrote a cover letter to the editor of the house to which he was sending the manuscript. He brought the letter down to read it to Carol while she fixed pasta for their lunch. She took the letter and sat down and reread it several times by herself. She said it was just right.

They refrigerated the pasta, packaged the manuscript and took it to the sub station to Express it to New York. They shook hands. Then they went to a bar and drank a toast to success. To contentment. To challenge. To love. And to each other.

They had hot dogs at a convenient stand near the lake, and they had soft drinks. They strolled hand in hand and talked about everything under the setting sun.

And they went back to her apartment, ate the pasta and went to bed to sleep. She'd obviously gotten over her fright from his book. The next morning when they wakened, he said, "Your terror has evaporated."

She nodded seriously. "You only really scared me the first time when I was worried about it fitting."

"That's all you think about—sex."

"Oh, do we speak of other things?"

"My BOOK!"

She sat up and opened out a whole arm as she inquired, "And?"

He chided, "You're calm again."

"I'm supposed to shiver and jump all the time for the rest of my life after one reading of your book?"

"Yeah."

"Oh. Well, I'll see what I can do about that." She shivered, but it was mostly shimmy.

He watched her. "You're a lascivious woman."

She was so surprised. "I've never been called that before now."

"It's just a good thing I came along when I did and thwarted your marauding the trembling ranks of men in this country. You would have wreaked havoc."

She commented idly, "How brave of you."

"Yes."

She started to move and said, "Ouch."

"What's the matter?"

"I have a crick in my hip from last night's tumble."

"I can rub it for you. Where does it hurt?"

She lay on her side, catty-cornered on the bed. She pointed to her hip. "There."

So he rubbed, and she moved in pleasure, and he watched. He smiled, and she was soberly as sinuous as a snake. And he spread his rubbings.

She put her arms up and stretched and rolled over and opened lazy eyes to be surprised she had his attention. Her mouth became a small O, and she used her hands to try to cover herself. He laughed.

She had no appointments.

Later, they went out into the early-September day and walked. Naturally, she took her sketchbook along. He watched people and eavesdropped, and the lovers discussed what people were arguing about. They didn't always agree how the arguments could be solved.

Back at the house, they watched the Cubs and commented they would have to get to the next game. The TV commentator explained one player had bad knees but just couldn't quit the game. He spent his time in therapy so that he could run. His determination made his knees work. He stole a base.

It was the third-base coach who signaled in an elaborate manner and told the batter what to do. And it was maddening to have the pitcher throw to first again and again and again, trying to catch a runner far enough off first base.

When a batter almost struck at a ball, the catcher and the umpire would ask for confirmation from the first- or third-base umpire as to whether the batter's stopped swing had been in time.

The viewers watched the new pitcher's wild pitches, which garnered a walk for the batter. And the rerun of a runner going into home, with the catcher waiting for the ball. The runner would slide slyly left of the plate, reaching out to touch home base at the last minute in order to avoid being tagged by the catcher.

The announcer would predict the change of pace by the pitcher, and there were the collisions of fielders who ignored the shortstop's call. Then there were those who

slid belly-down into a base and got the top of their pants
bands full of dirt, and they were discreet in emptying
them.

The TV even reran Ready running from first to second and jumping over the ground ball because, if it
touched him, he would have been called out.

Between innings, films showed how the batters sat
and watched tapes of pitchers who pitched cleverly. And
Carol began to know how skilled the men were who
played a "game" called baseball.

At those times when there was no game, the lovers
wandered all over Chicago, seeing things, noting, discussing and standing as she sketched.

His escorting presence gave her freedom. When any
male approached her, Tim was there. And he simply
loomed like any good policeman. She drew women so-
liciting so subtly that Tim was impressed. Carol said,
"She's a prostitute."

"Yeah." He watched the woman.

"With AIDS as life threatening as it is, I wonder at
anyone who is so rash."

He countered, "You were rash with me."

"You said you'd been pure enough."

"True," he agreed. "And you believed me."

"Why didn't you mention that then?"

"Because I was honest," he told her. Then he said,
"I'm grateful I've been as careful as I have. And,
honey, it wasn't very many times that I've been with a
woman. I had one serious involvement. We had never
been with anyone else. We were careful then, too."

"Who was she?"

He shook his head. "It doesn't matter."

"Why did you break up?"

"I'm not sure. I think she was distracted by another man. She lost interest."

"A foolish woman." Carol was emphatic.

"She didn't have your humor. I love your sassy tongue."

She stuck it out just a little.

He smiled as he looked down her body. He continued labeling what he liked: "Your slinky backside. Your wicked ways."

"I'm a nice girl."

"You're a sly woman."

"I've known you for over five months now."

Tim chided, "You ignored me most of the first two."

"Well, I've made up for it in just the last couple of days."

"Did I tell you I like sleeping in your bed?"

"Are you moving in?"

"Not altogether. I'll keep my apartment."

"You know I can't spend all this time playing. I have to get back to work. You distract me."

"I'm glad we've had these several days. I needed a companion to share my relief at having completed the book."

"It's done."

He cautioned, "It could be rejected."

"Why would *any*one reject such a good book? It's very good. Well done."

He smiled at her compliments. Then he said, "It could be different from what the publishing house has slated. It could be similar to another book. There are a lot of reasons, really, which have nothing to do with the contents of the book or skill of the work."

"Then you wouldn't be wrecked if it's rejected."

"Not entirely."

"You'd try another publisher?"

"Sure."

"You'll write another book?"

"Yes. I have to so that you can read it and get scared and insist that I sleep with you. Just getting to do that is worth all the effort of writing."

And she laughed at him. He was just wonderful.

But as they became closer and more involved, the nemesis became bigger for Tim. One day, any day, Carol could discover that her father had hired him to watch over her. What would she do? Already thinking like a teller of stories, his mind would weave scenes of her reactions to discovering what he had done.

Shock, anger, fury prevailed in his imagination of her counteraction. How mad would she be?

How could she ever trust him again? There was always the chance she could forgive him, but would she then trust him? That bothered Tim the most. When she looked at him, now, her eyes were filled with trust. There were no shadows of disappointment or doubt.

In October, there were two events that took precedent over everything else. The Cubs were to be in the World Series. And Carol's pictures were in the showing at the Art Institute. A lot of nerves were stretched. A lot of excitement was running rife.

Tim was slightly separated from the realities by a new book. Getting the sequence of events organized, making the plot flow, getting the zingers in place all distracted him somewhat from the pressure being endured around him, so he appeared fairly calm.

Just to be in the Institute's show was a high for Carol, and the reviewer gave her some studied positives. Nothing lavish, but the comments were positive. She was walking so high off the floor that she had to duck under the lofty chandelier.

The first time she stooped as she crossed the floor, Tim asked, "What's the matter?"

She asked, "Huh?"

"You looked like a bee was attacking. You stooped down for a couple of steps."

Quite seriously, she replied, "I ducked under the chandelier."

He gauged the distance up to the chandelier and considered it.

She said with a tad of impatience, "The positive comments by the reviewer has me walking that high off the floor."

Tim put his head back and blinked his eyes a couple of times then slowly, acceptingly, nodded a laboriously slow nod. He looked at his busy love and his heart melted. He had a lifetime with her to listen to all the wild things she'd suggest and communicate and try— depending on how mad she'd be when she found out why he was really there in that house.

How long would it take to smooth her ruffled feathers? Would she let him do the smoothing?

In an idle minute, it came to his mind, in a slowly filtering way, like toxic waste into a town's water supply, that none of the grad students had ever given Carol the time of day. They'd always been in a hurry or part of the party but they hadn't come on to her at all. That didn't make any sense.

They were her age. They were men. They liked women. They liked her and were cheerful friends. But not one had given her any rush at all. That was weird, and it niggled in Tim's subconscious.

He said to her, "Didn't any of the attic men appeal to you?"

"They're just like the kids at school."

Kids. She called them . . . kids. They were in their middle twenties. They were men. What did she mean, kids?

Then through shrewd eyes he considered Thelma. An actress. About Felicia's age . . . Carol had told of taking Thelma to meet Felicia, and Thelma hadn't said one word. She hadn't needed to, or she was not a good enough actress to fake not knowing Felicia?

Tim began to be shocked. What if. . . .what if all the people in that house HAD been put there by the Browns? The renters would live there just as he did. Each of those people in that house was in a position of his or her lives when they'd needed money for a while. They were all on the Brown payroll? Housed by the Browns? Ha! How ridiculous!

Tim found a time with each of the other residents to inquire casually, "How long have you lived here now?"

And he found that each had moved into the house in the late spring. Just before he had. Just before Carol had arrived.

He was supposed to be a detective. He was a little slow, wasn't he? But he remembered back to when he first saw Carol, and he knew he had never been reliable except as her guard. He hadn't paid any attention to any of the other housemates. One could have been Jack the Ripper. Naw. He'd have noticed something like that.

The lovers had tickets for the Series, and the October weather was brisk. They bundled up and went. Megen was entrenched nicely with Ready's family. They drank coffee, ate like pigs and yelled themselves hoarse. They left the park after the ninth inning, each spectator satisfied their yelling had helped the Cubs win the first game.

The second night was the same, and again the Cubs won. The spectators were all a little hoarse. That difficulty in speaking was like wearing a badge of courage.

And the third night, by golly, the Cubs won again!

But the bad part was that the Cubs would play the vital games at the enemy's field. Not everyone could take the time away from precious jobs and travel that far for just a couple of days. Vital days. Crucial days.

So with the third game won, the Cubs fans all stood up and gave the team a long, standing, yelling ovation. They left the stands reluctantly, and the Cubs' people allowed them all the time it took for them to leave.

It was very touching. It was like the night that it took the Cubs fourteen innings to break a tie. While there had been people who had gone to sleep on the hard benches, there were all the others who'd stood up along the seats, cheering and encouraging, and they'd stayed to the last pitch.

Cubs fans are loyal.

Tim asked Carol, "Do you want to go?"

"I can't. I have three people coming for sittings. I have to be here. It'll be on TV."

"You're not a native Chicagoan."

"No. I thought you knew I'm from Ohio."

"I did know. I'm just mentioning the fact that you're only a skin-deep Cubs fan."

"Is that illegal?"

"Practically," he assured her.

"I hadn't realized that."

Tim instructed, "There are a lot of details you must accept and acquire before you can call yourself a Cubs fan."

"Just going to the game doesn't do it?"

"It's a start," he soothed. "It's tough for an outsider like you. I'm a Cubs fan genetically, since both my grandmother and my dad were Cubs fans."

"I hadn't known it was genetic."

"I knew a guy who tried to switch to the White Sox. Couldn't." He slowly shook his head, looking out of the window at the blustery day.

"There's so much to learn in this world." She fretted. "How will I ever gain all the knowledge that I'll need?"

He took a deep, patient breath. "I'll do what I can with you, but I'll need your attention."

"Thank you."

"Not just casual listening," he warned. "I'll need your concentrated, involved attention. And I'll give you more shots."

"What . . . sort of shots."

He opened out his hands. "To help you become acclimatized."

"That's what you've been—"

"Why else?"

She was impressed. "I hadn't understood your complete dedication."

"I'm a dedicated man."

"How many incomplete women have you helped."

"You're my first." He was open and sincere. "You're such a challenge that I'll probably have to devote my entire lifetime just to your learning to be a regular Cubs fan."

"That awes me."

He grinned. "You're really a little unbalanced."

"Oh, but you are so convincing!"

"Don't pour it on too thick."

She batted her long lashes and said, "I just tremble to think of all the tall tales you're liable to tell our sweet, innocent children."

That sobered him. It wasn't the nonsense he'd pulled that bothered him, it was the truth he hadn't told that was eating at his conscience.

Tickets for the out-of-town games were hard to find, so television was the only recourse. The Cubs lost the first two games, but they won the sixth game to win the World Series! The Cubs were the acknowledged baseball champions of the world.

The acknowledged champions meant that while the Cubs fans had always known they were the champions, it was just that the rest of the baseball world now had the proof that they were.

Chicago was berserk with celebrations. It was a little like the fable of St. Louis after World War II ended. St. Louis had bragged on their days-long, open-ended celebration for almost fifty years. Now Chicago was the same way. It was like three New Years' Eves in a row. And everybody accepted it should be so.

"They won!" was said any number of times. Everyone instantly knew exactly who had won what. Seldom did anyone inquire, "Who?" or "What?"

Even people who weren't from this country knew who won what. Not even people getting off the planes from abroad asked, "What?" The pilots had informed the passengers of that crucial fact before they landed in Chicago.

The visitors were prepared. Some even said, "So the Cubs won." And there were probably some who thought it was some weird kind of contest between young bears. Someone actually mentioned bears, and the courteous reply was, "The Bears play football."

Not all people were courteous about the Cubs winning. Tim heard of one contract that fell through over the mistaken idea verbalized that the Cubs had been lucky.

All the players were heroes and there was a parade. The people were enthusiastic. Wrapped in the requisite fake furs of environmental protectionism, Megen got to ride on the back of a convertible with Ready. She loved it. Ready laughed. He saw Tim and Carol in the shouting crush and motioned them to come get into the car, but the whole mob tried to accept the invitation, and it was wild.

Someone had his foot stepped on by a police horse and raised Cain. Tim calmed him down and said, "Think, man, you can prove you was here!"

It was something to show to his grandchildren, a damaged foot.

But Tim got the limper through the crowd, along with Carol, and they found a first-aid station and got the man help. By then the man was bragging about being stepped on by a police horse at the celebration parade for the champion Cubs.

As they left the mob and wiggled their way into being able to breathe, Carol said, "You are such a clever man. You convinced that man he'd experienced an honor."

"Naw. I'm only human. I have to struggle along just like everybody else. I'm only a man."

"You suit me."

He was shocked. "You want me to put clothes on you? I've been working the other way around all this time."

"And you're impossibly irritating."

"That I can see." But he became unusually earnest as he cautioned her, "There might come a time when you would get really fed up with me. Then you need to remember only one thing. I would never hurt you. I love you." He looked at her very seriously.

"That's two things." She was sober-faced, too.

His voice was reedy with his emotion. "You're my life."

They kissed on the edge of all that maelstrom of cheering people, and some of the people around started cheering them. Then people started kissing each other. Then strangers kissed each other but, being cautious, that was just on the cheek.

It took Chicago almost a week to get over the buddy stuff brought on by the Cubs winning not only the pennant but the World Series. It was a rare and amazing time. Everybody talked to everyone else for a whole week.

But things got back to normal.

Ready and Megen were married at the farm in Porter County right after that and moved to Columbus, Ohio, where Ready was getting his degree in athletics at Ohio State University.

After seeing them off, Carol and Tim said goodbye to the other Farthingtons and began the drive back to Chicago. Carol said to Tim, "I'm impressed with the guys who prepare for the time that will come after their sports careers are finished. But do you actually think Ready could ever teach anyone else to be the athlete he is?"

"He'll try," Tim replied.

"Yes."

He asked, "When are you going to marry me?"

"Well, the last two Christmases, we've had somebody in the family get married. Two Christmases ago it was my brother, Bob, who married Jo. She's a great mechanic."

"Who was the last one?"

"My adopted brother, Rod. He married Pat from Fort Wayne, Indiana."

"I'm just guessing, here, but you want to be married this Christmas?"

"If you don't mind."

"I'd be honored." But his skin shivered over the fact that they would go to Temple, Ohio, just south of Cleveland, and he would be with Carol when they confronted Salty...and Carol would know about being set up by her own father.

And back at their house, a cheerfully innocent Carol went back to painting and drawing and watercoloring.

Tim began to ask the inhabitants of the house, "Did Salty give you any cash or did he just let you live here?" And the quizzed one replied readily enough, "Just the rent and utilities." But they added in variations, "It's been a godsend." Not one asked, "Who is Salty?"

Tim faced it squarely: Salty had set him up as Carol's husband. He'd calculated they'd be attracted by propinquity. Put together, the two young mammals of opposite sexes would become attracted and fall in love.

They'd been manipulated. She should know. She shouldn't be latched into a life and a man she might not really want. To be fair, he would have to tell her what had happened.

But she was invited to exhibit at another show. Then Tim received a call from New York and a rather formal man said, "We like your book. Do you have an agent?"

When the call was finished sometime later, Tim walked down the stairs and into Carol's studio. She was concentrated totally on what she was doing. He sat down and waited.

When she stood back from her easel, she glanced over at him and said, "You look . . . different."

"I'm an author."

"Yes." She went back to touching her brush to the canvas.

He said, "I've sold my book."

She looked up and began to smile. She said, "Wonderful!" She put down her brush and palette before going to him to throw herself against him and kiss him. They were exuberant. And she smeared him with some paint from her hands and chest. He didn't mind.

They went out to dinner and had some champagne, which neither particularly liked. Then they had a wine, recommended by their waiter, that was better. The two talked and ate and discussed and speculated and smiled and smiled and smiled.

Then Tim told her she'd been duped, not only by her father, but by him. Timothy Bolt had been a part of the scheme. However, he felt she should know that the scheme was a little wider than he'd first expected.

Carol listened, her eyes soft on her man. She nodded and was attentive—but she wasn't surprised.

He said to her, "You're not surprised."

"No. I suspected from the beginning."

"No! And you never mentioned it to me?"

"Mother told us about Sam Bolt when he died, and I knew you must be Sam's son. Why do you think I tried to avoid you those two months? But then you don't know about Bob and Cray."

"Your brothers."

"Yep. Bob was barely divorced and fired by his ex-father-in-law, when Salty and Felicia had Jo lined up to snare him."

"And he didn't suspect?"

"Not until it was too late."

"And Cray?"

"He was a restless man. He'd been traveling around the world, looking for something. He came home the Christmas Bob and Jo married. Mother and Dad sent him down to San Antonio to check up on a temporary guest we'd had, Susanne. They were married up here that summer."

"We didn't have a choice."

"No."

"You just reeled me in."

"Yeah."

"Are you going to be happy with me, Carol?"

"Deliriously."

"I think I can be good for you. I'll be a good balance."

"Balance? I'm female."

"That's the whole point—I'm a man. I can balance you."

"Under those conditions I, in turn, shall balance you."

"Yeah." He looked at her so tenderly, but he said softly, in apology, "You have to know I've suspected this plot for a while, but it didn't keep me out of your bed. And I never hesitated about wanting to marry you. I was just ticked to realize we'd been maneuvered."

"I can show you maneuvers."

"Why, Miss Brown, you shock me."

"I plan to."

She did try, in those precious years that followed, and, on occasion, she did shock him.

\*    \*    \*    \*    \*

# SILHOUETTE® Desire

MAN OF
THE MONTH:
1993

They're tough, they're sexy...
and they know how to get the
job done....
Caution: They're

MEN
AT
WORK

Blue collar... white collar... these men are working overtime
to earn your love.

| | |
|---|---|
| July: | Undercover agent Zeke Daniels in Annette Broadrick's ZEKE |
| August: | Aircraft executive Steven Ryker in Diana Palmer's NIGHT OF LOVE |
| September: | Entrepreneur Joshua Cameron in Ann Major's WILD HONEY |
| October: | Cowboy Jake Tallman in Cait London's THE SEDUCTION OF JAKE TALLMAN |
| November: | Rancher Tweed Brown in Lass Small's TWEED |
| December: | Engineer Mac McLachlan in BJ James's ANOTHER TIME, ANOTHER PLACE |

Let these men make a direct deposit into your heart.
MEN AT WORK... only from Silhouette Desire!

MOM93JD

Fifty red-blooded, white-hot, true-blue hunks from every State in the Union!

Beginning in May, look for MEN MADE IN AMERICA! Written by some of our most popular authors, these stories feature fifty of the strongest, sexiest men, each from a different state in the union!

Two titles available every other month at your favorite retail outlet.

In September, look for:

DECEPTIONS by Annette Broadrick (California)
STORMWALKER by Dallas Schulze (Colorado)

In November, look for:

STRAIGHT FROM THE HEART by Barbara Delinsky (Connecticut)
AUTHOR'S CHOICE by Elizabeth August (Delaware)

You won't be able to resist MEN MADE IN AMERICA!

## ANN MAJOR
## SOMETHING WILD

Take a walk on the *wild* side with Ann Major's sizzling stories featuring Honey, Midnight...and Innocence!

**September 1993 WILD HONEY**
*Man of the Month*
A clash of wills sets the stage for an electrifying romance for J. K. Cameron and Honey Wyatt.

**November 1993 WILD MIDNIGHT**
*Heat Up Your Winter*
A bittersweet reunion turns into a once-in-a-lifetime adventure for Lacy Douglas and Johnny Midnight.

**February 1994 WILD INNOCENCE**
*Man of the Month*
One man's return sets off a startling chain of events for Innocence Lescuer and Raven Wyatt.

Let your wilder side take over with this exciting series—only from Silhouette Desire!

## Silhouette Books has done it again!

Opening night in October has never been as exciting! Come watch as the curtain rises and romance flourishes when the stars of tomorrow make their debuts today!

*Revel* in Jodi O'Donnell's STILL SWEET ON HIM—
Silhouette Romance #969
...as Callie Farrell's renovation of the family homestead leads her straight into the arms of teenage crush Drew Barnett!

*Tingle* with Carol Devine's BEAUTY AND THE BEASTMASTER—
Silhouette Desire #816
...as legal eagle Amanda Tarkington is carried off by wrestler Bram Masterson!

*Thrill* to Elyn Day's A BED OF ROSES—
Silhouette Special Edition #846
...as Dana Whitaker's body and soul are healed by sexy physical therapist Michael Gordon!

*Believe* when Kylie Brant's McLAIN'S LAW—
Silhouette Intimate Moments #528
...takes you into detective Connor McLain's life as he falls for psychic—and suspect—Michele Easton!

Catch the classics of tomorrow—*premiering* today—
only from ▼ *Silhouette*

## WOLFE WAITING
### by Joan Hohl

This big, bad Wolfe never had to huff and puff and blow down
*any* woman's door—scrumptiously sexy rookie officer Jake
Wolfe was just too tempting and tasty to leave outside in the
cold! But then he got hungry for answers from the suspicious
lady who wouldn't let him two feet near her. What was a big,
bad Wolfe to do?

Huff and puff *your* way to your favorite retail outlet before
*Wolfe Waiting*—Book One of Joan Hohl's sexy BIG, BAD WOLFE
series—is all gobbled up! Only from Silhouette Desire
in September....

**Relive the romance...
Harlequin and Silhouette
are proud to present**

*by Request*

A program of collections of three complete novels by the most
requested authors with the most requested themes. Be sure to
look for one volume each month with three complete novels by
top name authors.

In June:  **NINE MONTHS** Penny Jordan
Stella Cameron
Janice Kaiser

**Three women pregnant and alone. But a lot can
happen in nine months!**

In July:  **DADDY'S
HOME**  Kristin James
Naomi Horton
Mary Lynn Baxter

**Daddy's Home... and his presence is long
overdue!**

In August:  **FORGOTTEN
PAST**  Barbara Kaye
Pamela Browning
Nancy Martin

**Do you dare to create a future if you've forgotten
the past?**

Available at your favorite retail outlet.

HARLEQUIN    Silhouette

REQ-G

Silhouette Books
is proud to present
our best authors,
their best books...
and the best in
your reading pleasure!

Throughout 1993, look for exciting
books by these top names in
contemporary romance:

**DIANA PALMER—**
*Fire and Ice* in June

**ELIZABETH LOWELL—**
*Fever* in July

**CATHERINE COULTER—**
*Afterglow* in August

**LINDA HOWARD—**
*Come Lie With Me* in September

When it comes to passion,
we wrote the book.

BOBT2